SHERLOCK
AND THE
EBONY IDOL

The Early Casebook of Sherlock Holmes

Book Three

Linda Stratmann

SAPERE
BOOKS

SHERLOCK HOLMES
AND THE
EBONY IDOL

Published by Sapere Books.

20 Windermere Drive, Leeds, England, LS17 7UZ,
United Kingdom

saperebooks.com

ISBN: 978-1-80055-735-2

To Izzy

From
Memoirs of a Medical Man
by A. Stamford FRCS

1924

CHAPTER ONE

When a man embarks on an adventure with Sherlock Holmes, he must expect danger. John Watson understood the risks and accepted them with fortitude, even relish, but I was not made of such strong material. Few men are. Nevertheless, I was always ready for the challenge, albeit with some trepidation. It will not come as a surprise to anyone familiar with the case of the Explorers' Club, that the experience left my nerves in a highly unsettled state. The police, for very good reasons, had advised us not to make the affair public; indeed, it was only after the passage of many years that I was free to publish my account. At the time, however, I did not have the solace of discussing it even with my good friend, classics scholar George Luckhurst. He was under the impression that I had been assaulted by a common footpad when the truth of the matter was far worse.

The result was that Luckhurst, who had recently started taking classes at a gymnasium, suggested to me that I join him and receive lessons in boxing from the proprietor, Professor Logan. Unlike the old days of the brutal bare-knuckle prize ring, glove boxing was a sport considered suitable for gentlemen amateurs who wished to take exercise and learn the noble manly art of self-defence. Luckhurst told me that if I became proficient and encountered the horrid footpad again, I should be able to deliver a sound drubbing, something I was disinclined to believe. On reflection, I think this may have been a humorous remark. However, I agreed to accompany him and see what the study of boxing could do for me.

Professor Logan was a bruiser of the old school. When I first met him in that winter of 1876, he was nearing forty, and claimed never to have been defeated in the roped ring, with or without gloves. Ten years before, he had given a good account of himself against the champion prize-fighter Jem Mace in a blood-spattered field in Kent before a howling mob of the gambling fraternity. Once the police got wind of the unlawful mill, they invaded the site, and every man was obliged to take to his heels. The match was declared undecided. Logan subsequently gave up the prize ring and used his winnings to acquire the tenure of a public house, the King Henry Tavern, in Covent Garden. He installed his brother as manager and converted the whole of one upper floor to a gymnasium. The tavern enjoyed a long-established connection to pugilism, hosting the meetings of London sporting clubs and providing lodgings for visiting professional boxers.

The King Henry was situated in a narrow lane which threaded itself between two busy and very different worlds, the teeming cluster of market stalls to the north, and the brilliance of Strand with its cafes and theatres to the south. As we drew near, we heard the noise of the public bar spilling into the street, a mass of conversations all battling to be heard, punctuated by bursts of loud laughter and the percussion of tankards. I sensed a convivial if somewhat boisterous atmosphere and guessed that any trouble if it were to arise would be very swiftly stopped. The gymnasium, I was glad to see, had a separate door, which we approached from the coach yard at the side of the building. It was not entirely possible to escape the din from below, which seemed to follow us as we ascended the stairs.

The gymnasium was a generous well-ventilated space provided with all the necessary equipment for a gentleman's exercise: there was an array of weights of all sizes, singlesticks, punchbags and gloves. A roped ring had been formed on a low platform in the centre and long wooden benches for the use of spectators were piled against one wall. The air was sour with sweat and liniment. Several men were using dumbbells under the professor's supervision, but when he saw us arrive, he left them to their practice and came to greet us.

Professor Logan was a fine-looking fellow, solid as a tree, with a broad chest that made extraordinary demands on his shirt buttons, and shoulders which would not have seemed too large on a horse. There were fine scars above his left eye and across his cheekbone which proclaimed his past. These, and the rough cord which bound back his dark hair, gave him something of a piratical air. I could feel only pity for any man who might choose to engage him in fisticuffs. Despite this formidable appearance, he was courteous yet quietly firm with nervous young gentlemen who were paying for his instruction. He seemed impressed when Luckhurst mentioned that I was a student of medicine, and observed that surgeons, if they chose, would make fine pugilists, since they knew where to do most damage.

My lesson began, and Luckhurst gazed on with interest as I donned a set of padded gloves and launched the fiercest attack I could manage on a stuffed punchbag. This was held steady for me by the professor, who did not appear to be inconvenienced by my efforts. After some instruction on the permitted blows used in boxing and how to parry them, Luckhurst and I were matched in some gentle sparring. The professor encouraged us not so much to try and injure each other but to aim for accuracy of strikes while avoiding being struck ourselves. Being light and quick on my feet I discovered a modest talent in that direction, although my unwillingness to cause any hurt to my friend did not play to my advantage.

As we refreshed ourselves with damp sponges and towelled ourselves dry, I commented on the impressive figure of our instructor. Luckhurst chuckled. 'I suppose you would like to see him in action,' he said.

'I certainly would, but I thought he had retired.'

'He gives public demonstrations of sparring from time to time. Next week there is to be a Grand Assault at Arms at the Agricultural Hall in Islington. Boxing, both competition and exhibition, wrestling, fencing, singlestick and so on. The professor will be showing his muscles there.' He saw my expression and said, 'I'll get tickets. He will also be offering a purse of £5 for any amateur who can last three rounds with him. I don't suppose you —?' He grinned.

'Not if he had one arm tied behind his back,' I said.

I had never visited the Royal Agricultural Hall, having no interest in exhibitions of fatted cattle and pigs, or those unbearably dull long distance walking competitions which the betting men, the Fancy, as they were known, once found so compelling. A display of martial skills was, however, considerably more tempting.

The day was dull and wet, but rather mild for the time of year. As the evening drew on there was a hint of mist, and when we arrived in Islington, feeling quite elegant as Luckhurst had insisted on hiring a hansom, there was a persistent cold drizzle. The stately brick and stone frontage that rose before us boasted two tall square towers flanking an entrance arch. We could see from the street that the extensive interior was roofed by a single magnificent span. Crowds of men, in heavy coats and mufflers, were already pouring into the hall. In the middle of all this movement, I saw an island of stillness. Three veiled ladies were gathered outside, and judging by the moisture clinging to their garments, they had been standing there for some time. They carried bundles of printed handbills wrapped in oilskin and were offering these notices to the men. Most of the men ignored both the women and their offerings or waved them away. As we approached the archway, one of the ladies, leaning towards me in an attitude of great earnestness, thrust a paper at me, and out of politeness I took it and put it in my pocket.

'Who are they?' I asked Luckhurst as we entered the hall and brushed a scattering of raindrops from our coats. 'They are fortunate the weather is no worse.'

'They appear whatever the weather at events such as these. I don't know their names. I call them the Furies. They believe that boxing should not be allowed. When they first appeared, they were initially suspected of being women of another sort and were arrested a number of times. The police now know them to be respectable ladies, if misguided, so they are simply asked to move on once they have distributed their handbills.'

I was soon distracted from considering this by looking at my surroundings. The great hall was said to be the most extensive exhibition place in London, capable of accommodating several thousand persons. It boasted a high arched iron and glass roof, supported by slender wrought iron pillars. The amenities included a refreshment room, booths for the purchase of tickets and reading matter, and a bandstand. The enormous space was made tolerably warm and bright by a generous provision of gas lights, placed around the perimeter, while suspended centrally above, there was a row of the largest circular arrays of gas I had ever seen, each with multiple burners. As the crowds assembled, the warmth of their bodies created a kind of odiferous vapour that further heated the air.

A platform had been erected in the centre for displays, part of which was roped off for boxing. There was ample seating in the upper gallery, but most onlookers occupied the ground floor where there were rows of bench seats behind low wooden barriers. The crowd was a surging mixture of enthusiasts of all ages, some clutching betting books filled with paper slips, and there was a good sprinkling of men of the press, already pencilling their first impressions. Premium seats were available at a price for the gentry in reserved areas, which were well filled. I could not help noticing one rather excitable little fellow who wore his top hat at a jaunty angle and jumped up to greet his friends as they arrived.

We collected a programme from a booth and took our seats, where we were briefly entertained by a small band of musicians at the rear of the hall. Professor Logan's challenge to amateur all-comers was the first item listed. A man in a well-cut suit armed with a bow tie and a speaking trumpet bounded into the ring and waved for silence. The music thundered to a halt, and after the usual greetings the host introduced the gentlemen who would be acting as referees and timekeepers for the evening, then announced the three-round challenge.

'Tonight, Professor Logan will be seconded by Mr Shem Logan, and Mr Morris will second the challenger. The professor is offering a purse of £5 to the man who can last three rounds, and the Marquess of Queensberry has promised to raise that to a total of £20.'

At this there was a burst of applause and the little man with the jaunty hat stood up and accepted the approbation of the audience. So, this, I realised, was the famous Marquess of

Queensberry, the young lord noted for his keen promotion of sport and said to be a good all-rounder himself.

Professor Logan entered the hall, and as he strode to the platform was enthusiastically cheered by the audience. He wore a loose flannel dressing gown, and once in the ring went through a few sparring motions. His second, who brought a water bucket and sponge, looked like a younger version of himself.

'Shem is his brother,' said Luckhurst, anticipating my thoughts.

'Does he box?' I asked.

'No, his wife won't let him.'

'Oh. Does the professor have a wife?'

'Several, I believe.'

The man with the bow tie looked about him and raised the speaking trumpet again. 'Come now, let us have a challenger!' The other second, an older gentleman who looked like he knew his business, waited expectantly in the opposite corner.

Shem drew the robe from his brother and there was a murmur of appreciation from the audience. Professor Logan now appeared before our eyes as a professional boxer. Stripped to the waist, he wore white close-fitting knee britches belted about his middle with a brightly coloured sash, white stockings, and leather boots. He was in fine trim for a man of his age, and I saw several of the more corpulent onlookers try unsuccessfully to draw their stomachs in as if that would assist them in matching him.

Just as I thought no man would be foolish enough to try his luck, I saw some movement from the audience. A familiar figure rose to his feet, leaped over a barrier, and stepped lightly into the ring, where he began nonchalantly to doff his jacket and loosen his collar. 'Holmes!' I gasped.

CHAPTER TWO

'Surely he doesn't mean to —?' I exclaimed. 'Oh, my word!'

Holmes, who, if he had noticed our presence was indifferent to it, began putting on a set of boxing gloves.

'I'm not sure I can watch!' I said. 'Have you seen the professor fight an amateur challenger before?'

'I have,' said Luckhurst, who did not appear to share my alarm at the prospect. 'He believes in giving a paying audience their money's worth, so it always lasts at least one round. He likes to take his time to size up the man, and so he merely toys with him in round one. Then, when we can all see it can't last, he takes pity on him and finishes him off in round two.'

'Finishes?'

'Oh, it shouldn't be too brutal,' said Luckhurst. 'But remember — Holmes boxed at university. I never saw him, but he was said to be very good.'

I felt a little more hopeful. 'He boxes in the sports club at Barts.'

'Then we should see a good bout,' said Luckhurst cheerfully, rubbing his hands together.

'What about round three?' I ventured.

'I'm not sure there ever is a round three.'

I had seen Holmes in combat once before, when he had defended us both from a street attack. On that occasion he was fighting for his life, and his opponents were undisciplined thugs, hired more for muscle than skill. This was very different. Logan was a scientific boxer in the style of the great Jem Mace, with power and precision in equal measure, perfectly combined, and I thought Holmes had too much pride to yield when he was beaten. I began to wonder about the spectacle of two men who were not enemies battling each other for no other reason than to amuse onlookers or to earn a purse. Perhaps, I thought, the Furies were not so far from the mark? I didn't know the answer.

The bow-tie announcer retired from the scene and the referee climbed into the ring. Holmes and Logan met in the centre at the place commonly known as the scratch and touched gloves. The referee issued the usual warning that he wanted a fair fight with no biting, gouging, kicking, or wrestling allowed. Then he stepped back, and the timekeeper sounded the bell.

It was soon apparent even to me that there were advantages on both sides. Holmes was younger and taller than his opponent with a noticeably longer reach. The professor inevitably outclassed him in experience. Logan at once tried the mettle of his challenger with sharp, quick and well-directed jabs. Holmes was fast enough to move out of the way or parry attacks on his gloves. He even contacted with one of his own blows, although Logan was able to use his skill to reduce its effectiveness.

When the bell sounded for the end of the first round, both men were well in the game and far from spent. I saw the professor give a nod of approval and respect for his young challenger. A quick lick of the sponge saw them both refreshed.

All too soon they were up to the scratch and facing each other in round two. The pace quickened and the professor's blows came harder and faster, often in rapid succession, impossible for the eye to follow. Holmes was severely pressed, and his face began to redden with the impacts, yet he did not give up as so many men might have done, and he even managed once to briefly enter under his opponent's guard and land a blow that saw the professor stagger back. It gave Holmes some valuable moments to recover his breath.

'Ah, the famous uppercut!' exclaimed Luckhurst as the crowds cheered the amateur.

Somehow Holmes managed to stay out of trouble for the remainder of the round, making short, rapid assaults with his long reach, but I had the horrid feeling that even the briefest lapse would see a swift end to the contest. The bell sounded once more, and both men retired to their corners for an extended interlude with a wet sponge.

I saw surges of furious betting activity in the crowds.

Round three began. Although Holmes was young and fast, Logan was still nimble, able to use skilled footwork to avoid being hit, and wisely wary of the uppercut. With a lesser amateur he would have been able to tire his opponent, and wear him down until he admitted defeat, but Holmes, for all his limited experience, was a natural athlete with superb stamina. The two men circled each other, breathing hard, the audience urging them on with loud yells. Then they closed and it was punch and parry, punch and parry as fast as lightning. Logan issued quick, strong jabs from the shoulder with a straight arm, Holmes managing to defend himself only with difficulty, while countering with blows of his own.

Then it happened. Logan took a large swing with his right which Holmes was easily able to avoid, but it was a feint, and the professor came in with a sudden left cross to the jaw. I saw Holmes spin and fall to the ground. The crowds roared, though whether in appreciation or disappointment I could not be sure. The referee stepped up to make the count, and I felt sure that the fight was over, but Holmes was not yet done. I saw him take deep breaths, gathering his strength. At the count of five he was on his knees, at six he got to his feet, at seven he faced his opponent and at eight he gamely raised his fists to show he was ready to continue the bout. He was clearly very shaken, and not fully recovered, but the referee stopped counting and allowed the fight to continue. Logan advanced for what I knew would be the final blow but before he could strike, the bell signalled the end of the round, and the crowds went wild.

Amidst the uproar we saw Logan take Holmes' wrist and hold his arm aloft, then clap him on the back. Queensberry bounded into the ring like a jack-in-the-box, shook Holmes by the hand and awarded the purse. The cheers were deafening. There was some brief conversation, then the challenger's second welcomed Holmes back to his corner and applied the refreshment of a sponge. Logan wrung the last drops from his sponge over his head, wrapped a towel about his shoulders, donned his dressing gown and jumped down from the ring, taking a seat nearby. Holmes left the ring to great acclaim and returned to his place.

When the audience was calm and settled again, the bow-tie man re-entered the ring. 'And for our next event we have a demonstration bout, and I will hand the speaking trumpet to our special guest this evening, none other than Bob Travers, the Black Wonder himself!'

There was a roar of applause and a sturdy dark-skinned man in his forties sprang into the ring and bowed.

'I think he was born in America,' said Luckhurst, 'but he's an Englishman now. Bare-knuckle in his day, he fought all the top men.'

'And now, gentlemen,' said Travers, 'I would like to introduce you to Jim Jones, a newcomer to London, who has come all the way from Cornwall to challenge Bill Summers next month for a purse of £50.'

The boxer who entered the ring and threw off his robe was a sight to see. Six feet in height, with muscles that appeared to have been sculpted to the most perfect ideal of manhood and gleaming like polished mahogany. He danced about the ring, light on his feet but with the promise of effortless power, and thew a few rapid sparring punches.

'I shall have the pleasure of acting as second to this young man,' said Travers. 'There will be a three-round demonstration, and his opponent tonight will be John Bowman of the Islington Boxing Club, who I am sure you all know well.' Bowman was a less imposing sight. He was strong and deep chested, but his muscles which were considerable in mass were not well defined, and his movements were slower and not so smooth as those of the young challenger.

'This should be interesting,' said Luckhurst. 'The professor thinks very highly of Jones, who is lodging at the King Henry. He could be a future champion. Bowman is older and may be past his best. He was never a true champion but has fought and won some hard battles in his time.'

A sparring match can be more valuable a spectacle than actual combat. It is an exhibition of skill, accuracy, and speed, and I determined to watch carefully to see what I might learn. I could see from the bell that the solid Bowman was outclassed by the younger man. Perhaps he had always relied on unrefined strength and durability. He moved in a flat-footed shuffle, his head thrust forward on a thick neck, and made little grunts as he threw punches. Jones was easily able to score against him, and I thought had it been a serious bout, he would not have found it hard to knock the other man down.

At the end of the first round Jones was hardly perspiring, but Bowman looked tired out and slumped heavily in his seat at the corner, gasping for breath as his second applied the sponge. There was something about the tilt of the older man's head that did not seem right to me. His second worked harder, then quickly beckoned the referee over to examine his charge. As the consternation in the corner grew, I knew that things had unexpectedly taken a bad turn. Jones rose to his feet with an anxious expression, Bob Travers went to look at the seated man, and Professor Logan jumped into the ring. There was a surge of muttering in the crowd. A steward was dispatched with orders to fetch a Dr Ridgeway, and Logan looked about him for more immediate assistance. I wasn't sure what to do but guessing that I was the nearest thing to a doctor in the vicinity, I stood up and raised my hand in case my help was needed. Logan saw me and quickly summoned me to the ringside. 'Bowman's fainted. Can you help him?'

Naturally I obliged. Bowman was unconscious in his seat, his body shuddering. He was a heavy man, with oily sweat cooling on his skin and his face a ghastly pallor. I did what I could to try and revive him while we waited for the doctor. On Ridgeway's arrival, which fortunately was only a few minutes later, I was content to act under the instruction of the senior man. Work continued, with the usual stimulants being administered. The insensible boxer was laid on his back, and we pumped his arms vigorously back and forth to encourage expansion of the chest. A stretcher was brought to the ring, and the bow-tie man peered over the ropes and told us that a cab had been summoned to take Bowman to hospital. During this interlude Jim Jones, who was visibly distressed at the unfortunate turn of events, made frequent enquiries about his opponent, repeatedly offered his help, and had to be reassured by Travers that everything possible was being done.

As Bowman was carried from the hall, everyone looked relieved, and the entertainment was allowed to continue.

'Was it a faint?' asked Luckhurst as I returned to my seat. 'Will he recover?'

I shook my head. 'It was no faint,' I said. 'The man is dead.'

CHAPTER THREE

Next day, Holmes was not to be found at Barts. There were no further classes that month, as the winter vacation had commenced, and most of the students were with their families or spending the season with friends. Holmes rarely did either. He had no experiments underway which required his supervision, so those students and lecturers who resided in London and were still about did not comment on his absence. I guessed that he was studying in his rooms until the marks on his face had subsided. I thought Professor Logan's speed and accuracy had tested him rather further than the gentlemanly sparring he usually engaged in at the Barts sporting club.

Bowman's body had been taken to Barts, so I was able to make some useful enquiries. As I had anticipated, the boxer had been pronounced dead on arrival at the hospital. A post-mortem examination was to be conducted to discover the cause of his sudden death. The man was only thirty-five. Mr Stevens, the examining surgeon, was a spruce, serious individual of about Bowman's age, who must have experienced more than the usual curiosity about the death. I told him all I knew of what had occurred on the previous evening: the demonstration of sparring, the collapse, and the strenuous efforts of both myself and Dr Ridgeway to revive the dying man. I really didn't think anything more could have been done. Since it was only a demonstration and not a fight, and I had been observing very carefully, I was sure that no dangerously hard blows had been delivered. The man had not been knocked down and his head had not been struck by anything harder than a padded glove. I had seen no symptoms suggesting a diseased heart. Stevens told me that Bowman had not previously been a patient at the hospital, and further enquiries had revealed nothing. The boxer had not recently consulted a doctor, neither had he taken part in a boxing match for several weeks or suffered any kind of accident outside the ring.

The London newspapers, fuelled by the scribblings of the ringside correspondents, carried reports of the incident, displaying varying degrees of accuracy, and the usual uninformed theories and speculation about the cause of death. Only the surgeon's scalpel would be able to enlighten us.

On the following day, Holmes, his facial redness somewhat faded, was back in the laboratory. I told him what I had learned and drew his attention to a letter published in that morning's *Times*.

There has been another horrible death from boxing. Yet another family has been cruelly robbed of its breadwinner. Death came quickly to Mr Bowman, but that is not always the case. A mortal injury may linger for many years, causing untold grief and hardship before it claims its victim.

Does anyone recall the sad fate of my poor husband Matthew Arroway? Let me remind your readers. Like so many young men who wish to provide well for their families, he was lured to the boxing ring by the promise of valuable prizes. Sadly, he was unequal to the brutal combat. He was matched in competition with a pugilist who battered him so badly about the head that he was never the same afterwards. At the age of just twenty-five, he was unable to work or take care of his family or even himself. My sister and I nursed him day and night for more than five years until his death last July. Had it not been for the kindness of others, we and my children would have gone hungry.

The much-touted new rules of boxing that have encouraged this so-called sport to flourish do not protect men against such a fate, as we have just seen. I do not blame Mr Jones for the death of Mr Bowman. He is young and therefore might not understand the risks and may not have been properly guided by those who have advised and promoted him. When will this horrid spectacle end? Must men who have no animosity towards each other punch themselves into injury and death? I do not disapprove of lively exercise which is beneficial to health, and there are many sports for those so inclined which do not result in fatal injury. If men must punch something, why not use a stuffed bag, where they might destroy as much oats and hay as they please?

S. Arroway

Holmes had nothing to say about the letter but a great deal about the night of Bowman's death.

'Bowman, as must have been apparent from the shape of his ears, was once a prize fighter of the old school and as much used to receiving blows as giving. He was a friend of the professor, whom I spoke to yesterday, and he told me that the man had fallen on hard times. That is a kind way of putting it. Boxing and beer, one often leads to the other, and they are a poor combination. One needs a sharp mind for boxing as much as any kind of sport worthy of the name. In fact, it was Logan who had arranged for Bowman to participate in the sparring demonstration to give him a little income, so he feels especially badly about it. The man had a wife and four children.'

'I didn't detect any smell of alcohol,' I said. 'He did give a few breaths before the end, and I think I would have noticed. I know that some men will take a drink to give themselves courage before a challenge, which is never the right thing to do. I would be very surprised if the post-mortem showed any evidence of it in Bowman's case.'

Holmes put aside the work he had been contemplating to give the question of Bowman's death his full attention. 'When you attended him, did you observe anything, any small and apparently trivial matter that struck you as unusual, that might have been the immediate cause of the collapse?'

I tried the best I could to recall the events of the tragedy in a calm, professional manner. 'There was nothing externally. Of course, having not seen the man beforehand, there might have been small changes from his usual state which I wouldn't have noticed. He was struggling to breathe, and clearly in pain and distress, but unable to speak.'

'The seconds and timekeepers have given their accounts and added nothing useful, and Surgeon Stevens has interviewed Mrs Bowman. She was adamant that her husband was in his usual health before he entered the ring. She did admit that he may have had a slight cold the previous day, but he appeared to be well again in the morning, and in any case, as she put it, no man has ever died from a slight cold. This is true, but Mr Stevens also told me something very curious. The lady was determined to blame her husband's death on young Jones, whom she said had a reputation for putting the "evil eye" on his opponents.'

'How extraordinary!' I exclaimed. 'But we must make allowances for a new widow who must be distracted by grief.'

'But there was something I saw that night,' Holmes went on, and he tilted his head back, lips pursed in thought. 'It was a small thing, which may mean something or nothing. I will not theorise further until we have the surgeon's report, but I did mention it to him, and he might find it will assist in arriving at his conclusion. The result will be crucial to young Jones. If it should be found that Bowman was, despite appearances, dangerously ill before he stepped into the ring, and might have collapsed at any time, whether he was boxing or not, then Jones cannot be to blame. If, however, the post-mortem should reveal that the death was due to some action of Jones, then he is in danger of being arrested and charged with manslaughter. There are many opponents of boxing who might welcome the publicity of a criminal trial.'

'But boxing isn't against the law, is it?' I protested. 'The old prize-fighting is, but surely under the Queensberry rules, it is allowable.'

'Allowed, rather than allowable, but competitive boxing has not been officially recognised in English statute or case law as legal,' said Holmes. 'Sparring with gloves, if properly conducted, is not considered to be an activity liable to cause serious injury and is therefore treated as legal. The old bare-fisted fights which continued without time limit until one man was unable to go on, is clearly not. But where is the line to be drawn between the two extremes? What of glove boxing for a purse, where injuries may occur, although both the number and duration of rounds are now strictly limited? The law has yet to decide. The police do not interfere with boxing if the rules are adhered to, but they can stop matches and make arrests if they suspect that the fights are conducted dangerously, for example if the gloves are insufficiently padded. Then there are individuals who are still wedded to the old ways, and claim they follow the rules to avoid prosecution, but flout them in practice. The police keep a wary eye out for them.'

As I digested this information, he went on, 'But I have agreed to keep Professor Logan informed as to what is learned here, and I will go to speak to him now. You had better come too, in case he wishes to question you.'

I was pressed for time, but the thought of Bowman's widow and children halted my objections and I accompanied Holmes to the King Henry. The weather had turned rather cold, and I saw that Holmes had put some of his winnings to good use with the purchase of a warm ulster.

'Professor Logan thinks you might make a tolerable lightweight if you were not so nervous of being hit,' commented my companion as we made our way. 'But judging by the assistance you rendered to Bowman, he feels you may have more value at the side of the ring than in it.'

I did not disagree. 'That was a fine punch he caught you with,' I said.

Holmes grunted assent. 'It was. I believe I learned more about boxing in a few hard minutes with the professor than in many hours with less demanding men. You have observed me employing my intellect delving into the darker impulses of humankind and will appreciate more than most that I need to have every kind of defence at my fingertips. There are desperate characters who would take exception to my activities and will seek to put a stop to them. The professor has suggested I take lessons from him, and I intend to do so.'

CHAPTER FOUR

As we approached the King Henry, I was concerned to see the three Furies standing outside, all thickly veiled and well muffled and mittened against the chill air and handing out their printed bills. I guessed that they had read the reports of the death of Bowman, an event which would have further confirmed their antagonism to boxing, and had made sure to discover where Jones was lodging. This reminded me that I had a copy of their publication in my pocket, which I had not yet read. I determined to look at it when I had the leisure. Displaying it inside the King Henry seemed inadvisable.

We went up to the gymnasium, where there was a subdued atmosphere. Several gloomy-looking men were performing exercises with singlesticks, displaying more than the usual determination, as if hoping this would go some way to their avoiding Bowman's fate. A young boxer, his hair clipped short like a brush, sat on one of the benches, head bowed. He wore loose exercise trousers and a shirt, and his gloves were unlaced. Lack of sweat suggested that he had not yet trained and was paused in the act of preparation. He appeared both nervous and dejected. The professor sat beside him, talking earnestly, and on the other side was an older man I had not seen before, nodding in agreement at the professor's words.

When we entered, Logan rose, came to meet us and introduced us to the two seated men. The young boxer was Bill Summers, the man due to fight Jones for a lucrative purse the following month. The other, Walter Robson, a grizzled veteran of sixty, was a retired pugilist. The professor spoke of him with considerable respect. 'I learned every trick I know from this man; he's fought the best.' Robson, we were told, had once been landlord of the King Henry before handing over tenure to the Logans. Retaining his affection for the house, he still lived on the premises, and was a valued advisor, helping with the training of boxers.

Holmes asked to speak to Logan, and he nodded. 'Not here. Let's go down to the office.'

We left Robson talking to Summers and retired to a small room at the rear of the ground floor, where a young lady wearing round spectacles was seated at a stool, managing some papers. When she saw us, she laid down her pen, smiled and hopped off the stool. 'You can have the office now, Calum. I've done,' she said, folding the spectacles and slipping them into the pocket of a chatelaine that hung from her belt, where they lodged amongst a collection of keys and other useful household items. She was a tiny, very slender lady, with brown curls and bright eyes, and I sensed a kind nature beneath the business-like manner.

'Thank you, Bella,' said the professor, warmly. He turned to us. 'Gentlemen, my sister-in-law, Mrs Isabella Logan, or Mrs Shem as she's generally known. Rules the bar and my brother and can add up numbers and get them right first time, which is a blessing.'

We exchanged the usual greetings. 'Bella, I just need to speak to these gentlemen in private,' explained the professor. She nodded politely to us and left us alone.

We sat down and told him how things stood with the post-mortem.

'Were you content that Bowman was in health enough to start?' asked Holmes.

A pained expression passed across Logan's face. 'I thought to help an old friend, and now I wish I had not. To be quite truthful, I would not have proposed him for a long bout, where he might have taken too much punishment, but I thought that three rounds of sparring was well within his capability, and both the activity and the money would raise his spirits. I insisted he should not drink beforehand, or I would not allow the contest, and he promised he would not.'

'His wife said he had a slight cold the day before. Did you see any sign of that?'

'No, he told me he was well.'

'He had not been previously injured?'

'Not as far as I know. At least, if he had, he had not told anyone of it. I saw no obvious injury, but then of course he might have been concealing one for fear that I would not let the match go ahead.'

'I noticed that the Agricultural Hall does not think it necessary to have a doctor in attendance at boxing and other martial demonstrations,' said Holmes. 'Is that usual?'

'As to boxing, the seconds know how to deal quickly with cuts, which are the usual injuries, and they have everything on hand they need. The referee will decide whether a man is able to continue. Dr Ridgeway's practice is close by, and either he or one of his partners can be summoned in a moment, as you saw.' Logan gave a wry smile. 'It was different in the old days of the prize ring, because we had to fight in out-of-the-way places to avoid the police. We used to ask a doctor, one in sympathy with pugilism, who we knew we could trust, to come and supervise the mill, as other help was not so near to hand, and the injuries were rather greater.'

'You know about the ladies outside, the ones who want boxing stopped?' I asked impulsively.

'I know of them. I don't pay any mind to them if they make no fuss and don't stop my customers coming in. They have their opinions.' He shrugged. 'Men fight. They will always fight. You can't stop them. Better they fight wearing gloves and under the eye of a referee than in the street with stones and knives.'

'There is a serious movement to discredit boxing, and any death in the ring will inevitably strengthen these ladies' efforts and attract others to their cause,' said Holmes. 'Have you read the letter in this morning's *Times* from the widow of Matthew Arroway?'

'I have been told about it,' said Logan. 'That was a bad business. I knew Arroway, but I never fought him. He didn't suit boxing. He was strong, but he didn't have the temper for it. He had all the confidence of the young, but none of the experience to justify it. He fought a man called Lunn, and was sorely punished, which didn't surprise me as Lunn at his best was hard to beat. I didn't see the fight, but those who did said that Arroway was knocked down by a single punch and struck his head. I don't know what became of Lunn. It was rumoured that he went to America to avoid the police.'

'Where was this fight held?' asked Holmes. 'Was it a reputable arrangement?' I could see that his interest had been piqued.

Logan paused and looked a little awkward before he replied. 'It happened in a room above a public house called the Two Spires, which used to host regular fights and pack the place with a crowd. I don't think the landlord paid much attention to the rules if he could get a large company and a good fight.'

'Would there have been a doctor on hand at that fight? Did he report the incident to the police?'

'It was a Dr Wrothby. He was a great lover of the prize ring. And he didn't have much to do with the police. In fact — well, I can say it now, as Wrothby is dead — I think the main reason he was employed to watch fights was that he did what was needed for the men and kept things quiet.'

'You mean he was trusted not to report a crime?' observed Holmes drily.

'That's about the size of it, yes. Wrothby went back a long way. Half the trouble of arranging a mill in the old days was making sure the police never got to hear of it, while the Fancy did. It had to be done by word of mouth, and Wrothby played a part in that. It was all about the betting then. There's still betting now, of course, but men like Jem Mace have shown us the science in boxing, and it's not just about brute strength and endurance anymore.'

That made me think of Bowman, whose forte must have been strength and endurance, as I had seen little of science in his boxing. 'Is anything being done for Bowman's family?' I asked.

'We have a collection box in the bar, which is already well filled,' said the professor. 'Our customers have been very generous. And there will be a benefit night.' He gave a sorrowful shake of the head. 'I am sorry for Jones, too,' he added. 'He is a good man, and a fighter with promise. He has a style all his own. In Cornwall he is known as the Black Falcon. They say he hovers over his opponent like a feather in the wind, then swoops in before they know it.'

'I hope that he will be exonerated by the inquest,' I said. 'I will probably be called to give evidence. I saw nothing to implicate Jones in any wrongdoing and am prepared to say so.'

'That is good news. He was very upset about Bowman, and it took much of the heart out of him. But even if it is proved he was not to blame, there are some who will refuse to accept it. I judge a man's worth by what he does in the ring, both by his skill and his attitude, and his conduct out of it. Jones has impressed me and others in the boxing world with his dedication to training and good manners. He is another Bob Travers; maybe he will even surpass him. But there are those who will be suspicious for no other reason than his colour, and I don't hold with that.'

'Mrs Bowman said something about an "evil eye",' said Holmes. 'Do you know what she might have meant by that?'

Logan smiled ruefully. 'Ah, yes,' he said. 'She must have heard the rumours about it. The ebony idol.'

CHAPTER FIVE

Both Holmes and I expressed astonishment at this revelation, and Logan went on to explain.

'Jones has a wood carving, made of ebony, I think, which he is very attached to, and carries around with him wherever he goes. You know how people are — they see a thing and imagine all kinds of stories about it. Some of the men are superstitious, and most won't go near it. They talk of it as some kind of African idol, and think Jones worships it, which is more than I have ever seen him do. They imagine it has the power to bring good fortune to the owner, and harm to his enemies. Even that it is the reason behind his victories in the ring. Some say it strengthens him and heals his injuries.' He shrugged. 'I don't think it is anything more than a wood carving.'

'I would like to speak with him,' said Holmes.

'Ah, well, he has gone to his room to be alone with his thoughts, which may not be the best thing for him. He needs to talk. I've not mentioned that letter about Arroway, as it wouldn't help his mood any.'

'What about Jones's match with Summers?' asked Holmes. 'Will that still proceed?'

'As you saw just now, Summers has lost confidence and we are trying to strengthen him with good advice. He is not afraid of the sporting challenge, but being one of the more superstitious men, he has got it into his head that Jones has special help from spirits. And Jones is simply too upset to think of boxing. If you put them in the ring right now, neither man would come near the other. And they are set to fight next month. I don't know what else we can do here. I'm hoping the post-mortem result will help some.'

'We may know the answer in a few days,' I said.

'But I will go up now and see if Jones is willing to talk to you,' said Logan. 'And then you may see the ebony idol for yourselves.'

'I hope it goes well for Jones,' Holmes reflected as we waited. 'From what I have seen of him, he is the epitome of the modern champion. The time is long past when boxing was little more than a battle of attrition. Oh, there were clever enough men in bare-knuckle days, but the rules of the ring have enabled boxing to rise to its true place amongst sports. You saw the practice with singlesticks? There is much in common between the art of fencing and scientific boxing. Mace also fences, as do I. The straight jab and the hook follow the same principles as the action of foil and épée. Logan and Mace have never studied anatomy, but they know where and how to place their punches.'

The professor returned in a few minutes with good news. 'He wouldn't entertain just anyone, but he is naturally interested in meeting my amateur challenger and the gentleman who helped Dr Ridgeway. Come with me.'

We ascended the stairs to the upper floors of the building, where there was accommodation for those who lived and lodged at the tavern. The walls of the corridor were adorned with prints of boxing subjects. Jem Mace featured, as did Bob Travers. There was also a portrait of Professor Logan in his younger days, formidable in fighting pose, with shaven head and bare fists raised.

The bedroom doors were numbered, and Logan knocked on the door marked three to announce our arrival. There were only a few moments of hesitation before a voice told us to enter.

The room was small and humble but cleanly kept. There was a narrow bed, a single gas lamp, a small fire glowing in the grate, the usual fire irons, a supply of coals and kindling, a washstand with bowl and jug, a large wooden blanket chest and a coat stand. The floor was simple bare boards partly covered by a small rug.

Jones, in his day clothes, was sitting on the bed with a bible in his hands, but as we entered, he put the holy book aside, rose to his feet, and greeted us. His height was intimidating but his manner was not.

'Mr Stamford,' he said. 'Thank you for all you did for poor Bowman. Dr Ridgeway said that no-one could have done any more in such a situation.'

I made some modest remark.

'And Mr Holmes, you impressed us all. I have not seen a better amateur.'

Holmes bowed his head in acknowledgement.

'Will you come up to the gymnasium and exercise today?' asked Logan. 'You must keep up the work. It will do you good.'

Jones shook his head. 'I don't know if I will,' he said. 'Perhaps when we know more about poor Bowman, it will help me decide what to do.'

'What prompted you to take up boxing as a profession?' asked Holmes. 'I perceive that you have worked as a metalsmith, although you have not followed that trade for some time.'

Jones looked surprised and even glanced at the professor to see if he was the source of that information. Then he stared down at his fingers, where there must have been some tell-tale marks which Holmes had observed. 'I — yes, you are right in both respects. I grew up assisting my father in his workshop. Like so many young boys who amuse themselves by fighting I took part in those games, and I did well. Boys who look different to others need to know how to take care of themselves. One summer, I was encouraged to try my luck at a boxing booth at a travelling fair. The professional told me I had promise and gave me the names of some men I should speak to. I am not sure my father was happy about it, but he gave me his blessing and said I could always come back to my trade if I wasn't successful. That was two years ago. Now, of course —' He sighed. 'I have written to tell my parents what happened before they read about it in the newspapers. They will be very upset and will probably beg me to come home at once.'

'Had you fought Bowman before last Wednesday?' asked Holmes.

'No, I had never met him. I knew something of his record, of course.'

'You saw nothing about him before the bout began that suggested he was in ill health?'

Jones gave this question earnest consideration. 'He seemed slow — tired — but that might have been his usual manner. I have sometimes seen men start slow on purpose, to put opponents off their guard, and then come in fast to attack. In any case, it was not a contest, just a demonstration of sparring. More like a friendly exercise.'

'Did any of you,' said Holmes very directly, 'and that includes you, Stamford; did any of you observe his legs?'

There was a silence, and we glanced at each other for clarification without result. None of us had. I felt a little guilty, as I ought to have observed everything about the patient, but of course when a man faints and is gasping for breath and needs reviving, one tends not to pay any attention to his legs. 'What is your theory, Holmes?'

He gave a thin smile. 'I will say nothing at present. A detail I observed at a dissection the other day has pointed me in a certain direction, but I will let you know once the surgeon has come to his conclusion.' He turned to Jones. 'Mr Jones, I would be extremely interested to see this wood carving of yours which has excited so much comment.'

'Of course,' said Jones readily. He opened the blanket chest and removed an object which had been carefully wrapped in a piece of linen. The chest appeared to contain nothing else, apart from the usual clothing and necessities. 'I used to put it on display when I came here, but it made some of the men feel uncomfortable, so I was obliged to put it away,' he explained, regretfully. He placed the figure on the mantelshelf and unveiled it to our gaze.

CHAPTER SIX

I am not sure what I was expecting as I saw the carving revealed — perhaps some hideous appearance which would naturally evoke terror in the onlooker. But the actuality was very different. The form was what artists refer to as a bust, representing the head and shoulders of a man. It was about a foot in height, almost as black as jet and very well polished. The face was long and narrow with a calm and dignified expression, the head quite smooth and bald. He wore earrings shaped like hoops, a decorative neckpiece, and a wrap folded about his shoulders, all these details carved into the wood. The base was embellished with cross-hatched lines.

'May I take a closer look?' asked Holmes.

Jones nodded assent and Holmes approached the piece for further study, taking out his magnifying glass. 'I am not familiar with this style of art,' he said, 'but I can see that it is not ebony as has been suggested but has been stained and polished to resemble it. The marks of the tools on the base, which have been used to create a pattern there, show that it is of recent make. The craftsman is undoubtedly very skilled.'

'My father made it,' said Jones. 'It was his gift to me when I came to London in the hopes of making my fortune here. He said that whatever I make of myself in future, I must never forget my people, my ancestors. The African has thrown off his chains and may walk with pride amongst other men, but we must always honour the struggles of those who went before. It has no power of itself, no magic. I am sorry that some people think it does.'

Despite the encouragement of Professor Logan, Jones could not be persuaded to do anything other than return to his contemplation. As he folded the carving in its cloth and laid it back in the blanket chest, we said our goodbyes and returned to our studies. I knew that once we had left, Holmes would tell me his theory if he thought it was worth repeating. He said nothing, and I did not press him to speak.

I was naturally eager to discover what Surgeon Stevens had resolved concerning Bowman. When Holmes and I went to see him the next day, he told us that the post-mortem was complete, and he was preparing his report for the inquest.

'Based on what I have found, I shall recommend that the jury should determine it was natural causes and nothing at all to do with the boxing,' he said. 'I can confirm that Bowman had not been under the influence of alcohol. He had taken some kind of tonic mixture, as many athletes do, but not in any great quantity and I am certain it played no part in his death. There was no injury to his head, no bruising to his body and no internal injury. His heart was sound.

'As you mentioned to me, Holmes, Bowman had the calf of one leg slightly plumper than the other, and importantly you observed this detail before the fight began. He had not told his wife about it, but there were traces of liniment on his skin which showed that it had been troubling him. Appearances of that kind in a young person can have many causes, most of them trivial, but for Bowman, that was not the case. I discovered some large blood clots in the veins of that leg. Small pieces had been breaking away and flowing towards his lungs. It explains the symptoms of breathlessness he thought was a cold in the chest the day before. It is quite possible that by the following day those small clots had dissolved, and he felt somewhat better. But on the day of the match, any amount of activity could have caused larger clots to break away and enter his lungs, and the heart was unable to receive blood.'

'Embolic patches,' I said. 'I have seen them in dissections, but only in much older subjects, and those in poor health. It is an unusual condition for an active man of his age.'

'I agree,' said Stevens. 'I can only theorise that he had an abnormality in his blood which caused the unusual clotting, but it is not possible to either determine or predict such a thing.'

We thanked him and Holmes was naturally eager to return to the King Henry and tell Jones as much as he was permitted to reveal in advance of the inquest. I decided to accompany him. It was another dull day, made grey and grim by a persistent misty rain that made the pavements slick with mud.

As we drew near to the tavern, we were surprised to see that a small crowd had gathered outside, blocking most of the lane. A police constable was busy trying to keep the thoroughfare clear for carriages, and another was standing in the doorway, preventing customers from entering.

'What's the to-do?' said Holmes. As he spoke, we saw two constables emerge from the building, together with young Jones. He was not handcuffed but was being held firmly by the arms. The boxer saw us and gave us an anguished look before he was quickly taken to a waiting cab. The crowds tried to swarm after him, making loud demands to know what had happened, which went unanswered. It was all the police could do to keep them back. Jones entered the cab, followed by the two constables, and the onlookers were obliged to scatter as the vehicle moved away. We tried to ascertain the reason for Jones's removal in this manner but learned nothing. There was a great deal of discussion and speculation in the crowds, none of which was to any degree informed and therefore of little use.

'Holmes?' said a familiar voice, and we saw Sergeant Lestrade, who had just appeared in the doorway. 'Is this a coincidence? What's your interest in this?'

'I came to speak to Jones about the death of Bowman,' Holmes explained. 'The surgeon at Barts has completed his examination, and he has just informed me that he will be reporting to the inquest that Bowman died of natural disease. I hope you don't plan to charge Jones with the death.'

Lestrade grunted and beckoned us closer with a tilt of the head. There was a step leading to a small entrance porch in front of double doors and we huddled there. Some of the onlookers tried to follow us and were firmly dissuaded. 'I don't want it bandied about,' he said, quietly. 'We may well charge him, but it won't be concerning Bowman. We think he may be involved in the death of another boxer who was lodging here, the man he was due to fight next month, Bill Summers.'

CHAPTER SEVEN

'But we spoke to him only yesterday,' I blurted out, a little too loudly, causing Lestrade to lay an admonitory finger to his lips before going on.

'Is that so? Then I suppose Inspector Sturridge who is in charge here will want to speak to you about it. And since you are both medical gentlemen, there won't be any harm in your coming in to see the body, so long as you don't interfere with the work of the police surgeon.' I may have been mistaken, but it almost seemed as if Lestrade gave a slight wink in Holmes's direction at that moment. 'The inspector is interviewing the landlord at present.'

He ushered us through the double doors, and as we entered, I saw Holmes give a satisfied smile. Looking back on that day, I think that even then he thought of himself not as a useful witness or informal advisor, but a consultant.

We passed through the main bar where there was a constable on duty, glancing hopefully at the counter and the barrels ranged behind it. Shem Logan and Mrs Shem were sitting at a table, saying nothing but holding hands. Three barmaids were seated around a table together. One was red-eyed with weeping, one was holding a handkerchief to her face, and the other, if she had been offering words of comfort to her friends, had given up that forlorn effort and was merely staring at them miserably. In the smaller lounge bar Walter Robson was slumped in an armchair, motionless, staring at an empty tankard on the table before him. The door of the office was shut, and I suspected that this was where the interviews were taking place.

As we ascended the stairs, I was expecting to be shown to where Summers had lodged but instead, we were ushered into room number three which we had seen before, that of Jim Jones. A fire glowed fitfully in the grate, and the lid of the chest in which Jones's possessions were stored was open. Stretched out on the floor with his feet pointing towards the chest was the corpse of Bill Summers.

I had seen death many times, of course, but scarcely anything as extraordinary either before or since as the sight which met my eyes that day. The features of Summers's face were contorted into a maniacal grin, the lips drawn back, nostrils dilated, the teeth clenched and exposed. There was bloodstained foam on his chin and the brows were drawn up into furrows of amazement. The body did not lie entirely straight as the spine was stiffly arched, the position of the legs distorted as if he had been engaged in a struggle. The most remarkable thing, however, was the ebony idol. The linen cloth in which it had been wrapped was lying on the floor beside the body. The carving itself was clutched convulsively in the arms of the corpse.

A grey-haired frockcoated doctor was standing by the body, writing in a notebook.

'Two gentlemen from Barts,' announced Lestrade.

'Ah,' said the doctor, closing his notebook. 'How convenient. I have done all I can do here, so you may remove the deceased.'

I realised that he had taken us for hospital orderlies, and made to correct that error, but Holmes motioned me to silence. He stood over the body, examining it dispassionately, then began circling around it, bending down for a better look, taking in every detail of its appearance.

'Do you know how he died?' asked Lestrade.

'That is to be determined,' said the doctor. 'Several possibilities come to mind. Fright, tetanus, or poison. You will receive a full report in due course. One thing I will say.' He picked up the poker and used it to lift the linen cloth by one fold, then draped it over the carving. 'Whatever you do, no-one must touch this object until it is proven to be safe. It may well be the cause of death. For what it is worth, my theory is that the deceased came in to steal it, but the owner, who I understand is from Africa —'

'Cornwall,' said Lestrade.

'Really? Well, in any case, he may have tried to protect his property by smearing it with some exotic foreign poison known only in —' The doctor made a vague gesture.

'Cornwall?' suggested Lestrade.

'Wherever his origins are,' was the testy response. 'I don't envy the examining surgeon trying to identify what it is.'

Holmes was kneeling on the floor at the head of the corpse. 'There is a small scratch mark on the back of the scalp,' he said. 'It appears fresh.'

'He might have clawed at his head in the agony of his last moments,' said the doctor. 'You can see the jaws are locked. It was a painful end.'

Holmes said nothing but frowned.

'We know that the man was last seen alive about three hours ago,' said Lestrade. 'He was in his own room then, the one next to this, number four. Professor Logan spoke to him and suggested he come up to the gymnasium, as the men of the Covent Garden Boxing Club had come to exercise, but he said he would not. Jones did go, and when he returned to his room, he found the man lying there dead and gave the alarm. Can you estimate when he died?'

'The body is still fairly warm to the touch.' The doctor reached over and thumbed back an eyelid. 'Some clouding of the eyes. Between one and three hours ago. That is all I can say.'

'There are enough witnesses to show that Jones was not in this room when Summers died,' said Lestrade, 'but then, if your suspicions are correct, he didn't need to be.'

The doctor pocketed his notebook and pencil. Glancing at us, he said, 'I hope you have brought a stretcher.' Then, taking up his medical bag, he left the room.

Holmes took out his magnifying glass and began what I now recognised as his typical thorough examination of the body and its surroundings. He studied the rug, where there were specks of dried mud, and Summers's boots, taking a sample of earth from the soles and placing it in an envelope, then he inspected the fireplace and the irons, and the contents of the blanket chest. He looked at the man's hands, especially the fingers, with great care, then, using the poker to lift the linen cloth, he passed his glass over the idol.

'Holmes, when you visited here yesterday, I know you looked at the idol, but did you touch it?' I asked.

'No, it is well-polished, and I thought my finger-marks would not improve it.'

'And Jones, did he touch it when he unwrapped it?'

Holmes straightened up. 'My recollection is that he removed it from the chest, where it lay swaddled in linen like a babe, set it on the mantelshelf, and then drew the cloth away. I can detect a slight odour of liniment on Summers's fingertips, and no doubt the surgeon will discover what part of his body was troubling him, and there are many marks on the carving, most likely with traces of that same liniment showing that Summers clutched it not once but several times. He now has it pressed hard against his chest. I do not believe that the scratch on the scalp was inflicted by the deceased. It is not deep, and has not bled a great deal, but if he scratched himself, I would expect to see some evidence on his nails, traces of blood or skin, and there are none. Also, the fingernails are cut very short. They could not have made that scratch. I do, however, see a smear of blood on the rug where his head has brushed it.'

'It is in rather an unusual position on the back of head,' I said. 'Could he have been struck by a weapon of some kind?'

'There is nothing present that could have caused it.' Holmes completed his inspection of the room and its contents, but there was nothing further to discover. 'If Jones had some secret poison to smear over the idol, I see no sign of any,' he said.

'He might have thrown it away,' said Lestrade. 'I'll have the dustbins searched.'

'Even if he had,' I said, 'surely the fault was Summers's for trying to steal.'

'He must bear some of the blame,' said Lestrade, 'but just imagine if someone had simply picked it up out of innocent curiosity, with no intent to steal. If Jones had protected it with poison and not told anyone then he has been negligent, perhaps criminally so, and a jury might find him guilty of manslaughter. If he intended to harm anyone who touched it, then it's murder.'

CHAPTER EIGHT

Holmes thought about Lestrade's worrying conclusion and shook his head. 'Jones agreed to let me examine it and he did not warn me not to touch it,' he said.

'He might not have known how dangerous the poison was,' said Lestrade. 'Or he might have smeared it on after your examination. All I'm saying is, things could go hard with him, especially after Bowman's death.'

'But that was not Jones's fault,' I protested.

'I don't know,' said Lestrade, shaking his head dubiously. 'Seems like too much of a coincidence to me.'

At that moment, the orderlies arrived from Barts with a stretcher to remove the body, and Lestrade made sure to repeat the doctor's instructions not to touch the ebony idol. Faced with a grinning corpse clutching an unusual carving, they appeared eager to take the warning seriously.

Holmes was lost in contemplation as the body was borne from the room. Although he was outwardly calm, I believe that he was deeply impressed by what he had seen. He cannot have failed to know the medical implications of the horrid grin, but these things were not as precisely understood then as they are now. Then and even in later years, he could not help but see some additional emotional element in the immediate history of the deceased in what doctors call *risus sardonicus*.

Lestrade watched anxiously as the body was manoeuvred down the narrow stairs. 'Of course, if you think the doctor's theory to be a little strange — and don't deny it, I saw you did — then even more peculiar is what Walter Robson told us earlier. He's the man who used to have the tenancy of this place, and he still lives here. You wouldn't credit it, but he insisted that Summers was killed by a ghost.'

'Indeed, did he name the ghost?' asked Holmes, more in jest than interest. 'Or was it just a white lady who appears at the bottom of a brandy glass?'

'He said that it was the spirit of a Doctor Wrothby, who was a regular customer here for some years. The few times I encountered him, he was more of a nuisance than anything else. The best you can say about him is that he was a great lover of pugilism and went to all the fights and treated the boxers for cuts and bruises, no questions asked. But he liked his drink too much. When he was in his cups it made him challenge them all to a fight, which was not very sensible, as they were half his age and twice his size and could have blown him over with a puff of air. Many's the time the constables went in to see what all the fuss and noise was about and had to calm things down. Another tavern would have stopped him coming in, but out of recognition of all he'd done for boxers in the past, he was tolerated here. One night, he was roaring drunk as usual and drove off home in his chaise. Next morning, his wife found him outside the house, still sitting in the chaise, reins in his hands, stone dead. It was a cold night, and he must have been chilled to death. Anyhow, Robson claims he sometimes sees the ghost of Wrothby, usually in the public bar where he liked to sit with the boxing men, demanding a drink and challenging all and sundry to a fight.'

Holmes chuckled. 'Does anyone else see this belligerent spirit?'

'I think the only spirits are what Robson indulges in. But he claims that Summers must have seen Wrothby's ghost, and the fright stopped his heart.' Lestrade shivered. 'I don't hold with ghosts. Give me a ruffian with a knife or a gun and I know where I am with him. Ghosts can be anything they like.'

Holmes did not look inclined to pursue that line of enquiry. 'Show me where Summers was lodged,' he said.

Lestrade obligingly took us to the next room, which was very like the one Jones had occupied, with amenities which included a narrow, low wardrobe and a small chest of drawers. The bedsheets had been drawn back right to the foot of the bed, and a thin coverlet was rippled into folds on the floor. The fire had burned down in the grate and there was an assembly of grey coals, cloaked in debris. Holmes carefully examined the contents of the grate, noting that it included fragments of rough kindling and blackened newspaper. One item caught his attention, a tiny splinter of wood. It was on the edge of the grate, where having missed falling into the fire, it had lain and become charred. He took a notebook from his pocket, tore out a page and eased it underneath the splinter to lift it, then folded the paper over and placed it in an envelope. Holmes then examined every item in the room, including the arrangement of the bedclothes, and crawled carefully over the floor, studying the surface minutely.

When he finally stood, he was silent for a while.

The door opened abruptly, and a police inspector entered. 'Lestrade? You're wanted downstairs.' He stared at us. 'Who are these men?' he demanded.

'Ah, Inspector Sturridge,' said Lestrade. 'Let me introduce you to Mr Holmes and Mr Stamford. As you know, they have given valuable assistance to the police in previous cases.'

The inspector, a broad-shouldered man in his fifties, was clearly unimpressed by these credentials, and uttered a weary sigh. 'I have no use for meddling amateurs. What are they doing in this room? It's already been searched.'

'Indeed?' said Holmes. 'Including the arrangement of the bedclothes? Have they been disturbed by your men? Or left as they found them?'

'There's nothing in the bed,' said Sturridge. 'But never mind that. Please go, gentlemen, unless you are witnesses to the crime and have anything to say?'

Holmes refused to be ruffled. 'If we may be permitted, my young friend is somewhat disturbed by seeing the body of poor Summers. I would like to provide him with a glass of water. Mineral water, if the premises can provide it.'

I did my best to appear disturbed. I admit I was a little peeved at being described as a 'young friend' as Holmes and I were the same age, although I understood his reasons. With the passage of many years, my relatively youthful appearance has of course become a matter of quiet pride.

The inspector snorted with annoyance. 'One glass, if you must. Downstairs, but do not stray from the public bar, do not impede the work of the police and once you are done, take your leave.'

Holmes simply gave a slight bow, and we withdrew. I could see that he was disinclined to argue with a disgruntled police officer. He preferred to take his revenge in his own time, by revealing the facts of the case which the officer had missed.

We went down to the main bar. The barmaids had gone, and only Shem Logan and Mrs Shem remained. Lestrade told the constable on duty that we were to be allowed to stay. 'The inspector isn't a bad sort when you get to know him,' he told us. 'But he likes to abide by the rules. So, you saw Summers yesterday?'

'Yes, when he appeared in good health, although apprehensive about the forthcoming match. But you will already know that from Professor Logan and Mr Robson, who were both talking to him.'

Lestrade made a note. 'I'll mention it to the inspector, in case he wants to speak to you, but I doubt it. Anyhow, I must go and see that the people outside are moved out of the lane before they cause any more of a nuisance. Ladies especially. Not right to have them standing there. Some of the men can get the wrong idea.'

As Lestrade bustled away, I saw Mrs Shem Logan give him a sour look.

'If I might have two glasses of mineral water,' said Holmes.

Mrs Shem rose to comply with the request but looked us up and down, trying to weigh up who we might be. She had not been suspicious of us at our last brief meeting, but our admission to the premises when customers were being kept out while the police were brought in, had made her wonder.

'That's all right, we are not police,' said Holmes, who could be quite engaging with ladies when it suited his purpose. 'We study medicine and chemistry at Barts and exercise at Professor Logan's gymnasium. And we have a special interest in the prevention of harm from competitive boxing.'

Holmes had judged the lady correctly, for Mrs Shem at once looked on us more favourably.

'As to that, you want to speak to a friend of mine, Mrs Arroway,' she said. 'Her husband died from boxing. She is one of the three ladies who go about preaching the word against pugilism.'

'And very respectably they conduct themselves,' said Holmes. 'I commend their courage and good sense.'

When the two glasses of water were filled, Mrs Shem offered a surreptitious touch of brandy to them and we did not refuse.

She took our glasses to a table, and we made ourselves comfortable.

'I have viewed the body of the unfortunate Mr Summers,' said Holmes, in the assured manner of a professional consultant, 'and I think it will be some time before we discover the truth behind that tragedy.'

'I am still waiting to be called to speak to the inspector about that, but I have nothing to tell him,' said Mrs Shem. 'I didn't really know poor Summers. He had only lodged here a few days, and whatever happened, it was as much a surprise to me as anyone.'

Holmes looked disappointed, and Mrs Shem was about to return to the bar counter when he asked, 'Did you know Mrs Arroway's husband?'

'Only after he was injured,' she said. 'That sad business was five years ago, before I married Shem. I first met Susan Arroway when I found her weeping in the street after she heard his doctor had died. She was devoted to her husband. She and her sister Jenny — Miss Mitchell — they had to share looking after him and the two children, doing what work they could to put food on the table. I used to go round sometimes to help them out with what we had left in the larder. And the boxing club used to send them something as well. It's only down to Susan and Jenny that her husband lived as long as he did. But he finally passed. It was only a few months ago. The children are at school, now, and a credit to the family. These days, Susan and her sister spend all the time they can spare telling people about the dangers of boxing. And their friend Mrs Goode goes with them. She is a doctor's wife, so she knows more than most.'

'I assume there is no doubt that the death, even so long afterwards, was due to the injury he suffered in the boxing ring?'

'None at all. And the man who killed him has gone away who knows where. It was a nasty fight, I was told. Susan thinks that man meant to injure her husband, not as sport, but in malice. It was no accident, not even manslaughter. It was cruel, determined murder, and that's a fact.'

CHAPTER NINE

The word 'murder' never failed to engage Holmes's attention. This was not, I hasten to add, a prurient interest. He did not delight in the misfortune of others. It was a matter of pure intellect. Holmes was excited both by the prospect of an unsolved mystery and an event which would afford him greater understanding of the darker realms of the human mind.

'Professor Logan has already mentioned the Arroway fight to me, although he did not see it himself. He told me that the other man was called Lunn, and it was at the Two Spires, was it not?'

'Yes, Castle Street, Soho,' Mrs Shem said, appearing a little surprised that Holmes knew that much. 'It was before Calum had this place. He was still boxing then, earning the purses that paid for the licence, and he was away in Liverpool or Manchester or somewhere like that.'

'But it is obvious to me that someone who saw the fight must have told him about it. I would be extremely interested in meeting that person for a discussion. It would be of immeasurable assistance in my study of the dangers of boxing.'

Mrs Shem hesitated. I could see she was struggling with a determination to say nothing more. Holmes stared at her searchingly, as if her face was a book and he was reading it for information.

'I really think that anyone who was present would be most unwilling to talk about it now,' she said at last.

'Even an innocent spectator?' asked Holmes. 'Your husband, perhaps. He might have gone there to watch in order to report back to his brother. How can he be blamed for that? I shall ask him.' Holmes made to rise from the table. If it was a guess intended to test the water, it hit the mark.

'No! Please!' she exclaimed. Holmes sat down. Mrs Shem took a deep breath before she continued. 'Shem was not a spectator of boxing. He was at the Two Spires because he worked there, at the bar. He doesn't like to talk about that night. He told me about it once, but he has never mentioned it since. But it's still there in his mind.'

She looked around at Shem, who was standing behind the bar counter, polishing tankards. The resemblance between him and his older brother was apparent; the same height, solidity of build and dark hair, but while the professor moved with a bold, confident air, his brother had an altogether gentler, almost timid pace.

'I don't want him upset. If he is, he'll say nothing at all. But if you promise not to question him, I will tell you everything I know.'

'Please do,' said Holmes.

She glanced about the room. The only policeman was not in earshot, and she finally sat down, pulled up her chair as close as it would go, folded her little hands, and rested them on the tabletop.

'Your husband is not a boxer?' asked Holmes.

'Shem,' she said with an affectionate smile, 'well, you've seen him — he is big and strong like his brother, but he doesn't have the quickness. Doesn't know his right hand from his left half the time. I told him he'd better not, he'd get hit too easy, and I don't want his nice face all cut up. Calum agreed he wasn't suited to it. Shem doesn't mind. He has no ambitions that way, and he likes bar work. Slow but steady, that's him. The nearest he comes to boxing is seconding Calum.'

'But he witnessed how Matthew Arroway was injured?'

'Yes. The other man, Lunn, he was an older man with a lot of fights behind him. Matthew Arroway was young — he wanted to prove himself, find a man to arrange the best matches, make a name. There was a lot of interest that evening, and Calum would have been there to watch if he had been in London. But when Lunn arrived, he was in a shocking state. He'd been drinking and he'd had a fall in the street on the way there and hurt himself. There was a cut on his forehead and his face was all covered in blood. Shem didn't think he was fit to go in the ring, but the landlord, his name was Meaney, he wanted the fight to go on or he'd lose money. There was this doctor — and he was no stranger to drink, either.'

'Dr Wrothby?' suggested Holmes.

'Yes, that was the man. Meaney asked him to take a look at Lunn, and he said the cut was nothing to speak of and put a bandage on it. Shem was sent to make hot coffee and Lunn was made to drink it to sober him up, and then Wrothby said he was fit to fight. Calum said later that if he had been there, he would have put a stop to it.'

'If I had been there, I would have called the police,' I said, appalled that such a spectacle should have been permitted.

'I don't think there was anyone there willing to go that far. Shem stayed and watched from the back in case he was needed, and he was sorry he did. When the fight began, it was obvious to everyone that Lunn was drunk. Arroway — he thought it was all a joke. He didn't even try to defend himself. He must have thought Lunn was too slow to hit him. The crowds began to jeer and then Lunn punched him with all his strength, and he went down. Shem said that Lunn's punch was so hard he even hurt himself, and Wrothby had to bind up his wrist. But Arroway was out before he hit the floor. He fell directly onto his head, and then he just lay there.'

'And Wrothby attended him?'

'Yes.'

'Was he taken to hospital?'

'Oh, no. Shem begged Wrothby to take him there, but Meaney wouldn't allow it. He was carried home, still unconscious. Poor Susan had the shock of her life when she saw him in that state.'

'It seems to me that Meaney and Wrothby were the men most to blame,' I said.

'Well, Wrothby is dead now, and I heard that Meaney is too. No-one knows where Lunn is. And anyone else who was there is not admitting it. But in my opinion, Lunn went into the ring drunk and hit a man who didn't even have his fists up to defend himself. He should take the blame. Arroway didn't try to fight a drunken man, he had more respect for himself than that, but he taunted him, and the crowd did too, so when Lunn hit an unguarded man, he did it from anger, not sport, and meant to hurt him. That's murder, to my mind.'

'I should have liked to speak to both the landlord and the doctor,' said Holmes regretfully.

'Wrothby never talked about his part in it, even when he was in his cups. He used to say he had a thousand tales to tell that might bring people to shame, but he never did.'

'Mr Robson claims to see Wrothby's ghost,' I said.

'He does, but he's the only one,' said Mrs Shem. 'If there are ghosts in this tavern, they are in people's memories. Robson saw a lot in the time when he was landlord. He still mourns his poor wife, who died here many years ago. She had a long, painful time of it.'

'And Matthew Arroway? How did he fare when he was brought home? Did he regain his senses?' said Holmes.

'Yes, but he was never the same man. He had strange ideas, bad tempers, pains in the head. There was nothing anyone could do for him. He died in the night — the doctors said it was blood in the brain. It was a mercy to all of them. Susan was so devoted to him and the children. Jenny — she once had hopes of marriage but gave that all up.'

'I can see why Mrs Arroway and her sister feel that boxing should be stopped,' I said.

'Susan once told me that she never really liked it, even before that fight with Lunn, but she let her husband do what he wanted, hoping he would make enough money to give it up and start some better occupation that would see them comfortable. But Jenny —' Mrs Shem gave a little smile. 'Now, she only turned against it afterwards. She was engaged to be married once. Billy Blunt was his name. He was a big fellow, the son of a local butcher, and a boxer. He fought under the name Butcher Blunt. But after what happened to her poor brother-in-law, Jenny never liked boxing again. The engagement was broken off, Blunt went and married another and is now a father of three.'

At that moment, the professor arrived, with a serious expression. He went to the bar, poured himself a glass of brandy, threw it down his throat as if it was nothing, then refilled the glass, picked up the bottle, and came to our table.

Mrs Shem decided to go and help her husband with the cleaning and tidying. She joined him behind the counter, rinsed and wrung out a cloth in a water bucket, and began to wash down the shelves. The couple said nothing to each other as they worked, but it was a sympathetic, companionable silence.

'Bad business,' said Logan, flinging himself into a chair, 'especially after this last affair.' He sipped his drink, thoughtfully, and was kind enough to offer us some, but we declined. 'Mr Holmes,' he went on, 'Sergeant Lestrade has told me something about you which interests me. He says that you are a man who likes to solve mysteries for his own amusement. He even said that you have given the police a few clues which have helped them in the past. Is that so?'

'Oh, concerning one or two trivial matters, yes,' said Holmes, the master of false modesty.

'I wondered, would you be willing to look about you and see if there is anything in the question of Summers's death with might help young Jones? I can't imagine he is to blame in any way, but if he was to be suspected of a crime it might prove hard for him.'

'I will certainly do so,' said Holmes.

'If anyone employed here objects to your questioning them, just refer them to me. Oh, and in recompense for your trouble, I can provide some additional boxing lessons if that would suit.'

So it was that the first earnings of Sherlock Holmes as a professional detective came in the form of boxing lessons.

'In that case, I shall commence my enquiries immediately,' said Holmes. He did not stir from his chair, and it was a moment or two before Logan realised that he was to be the subject of Holmes's first interview.

CHAPTER TEN

'Do you know who the last person was to see Summers alive?'

'That might well have been me,' said Logan, who appeared perfectly comfortable with that admission. 'He was supposed to be in hard training for the match with Jones. But when he didn't come to the gymnasium, I went to see him.'

'What time was this?'

'It would have been just after the afternoon classes began. We start at two o'clock. I must have gone to speak to him soon after, when he didn't appear, maybe ten minutes past. He was in his room, sitting on the bed and looking very unhappy, nervous, even fearful. I asked if he was coming to train, and he said he didn't have the heart for it. I told him he had nothing to be afraid of if he was properly prepared for the match, that he was a good man and knew how to handle himself, and Jones always fought a clean, fair fight. He said he had nothing against Jones, as a man or a boxer, but he thought that Jones was protected by some sort of magic.' Logan shook his head in exasperation. 'I tried to reason with him, but it did no good, and I gave up as I had to go back to take a class. I told him he should come up and train as soon as he felt able, as the exercise would do him good. He said he would try, but from his manner I didn't expect to see him in the gymnasium. I wasn't surprised when he didn't come.'

'How long were you speaking to him?' asked Holmes.

'Only a few minutes. When the classes ended at four o'clock, I went to look for him, but he wasn't in his room. I thought he might have gone out to get some air and take a little run. The men often run, it's good for the wind. They do it in all weathers, and a little rain keeps them fresh. It was only when Jones went to his room that Summers was found dead there.'

'When you spoke to Summers, you say he was sitting on the bed. Were the bedclothes tidy or in disarray?'

Logan looked surprised by the question. 'I can't say I noticed in particular.'

'The cover was not lying on the floor?'

'No, I think I would have noticed that.'

Holmes nodded thoughtfully. 'The police must have moved it when they searched the bed. What about when you returned to Summers's room to look for him after the class? Did you notice anything unusual? Something that was different from two hours before?'

'You ask some hard questions, Mr Holmes,' said Logan with a smile. 'I suppose that is how you solve mysteries. Well, now you mention it, the bedclothes were a little rumpled, and I did think for a minute, the sly dog, he has only pretended to be unsettled, and has taken the opportunity to have a woman in here. He was always rather shy around women, although I heard that one of the barmaids had taken a fancy to him, so you never know. If you ask them, you might find out more.'

Holmes looked displeased, and I suspected that from considerations of propriety he was uncomfortable about the prospect of interviewing barmaids about such an indelicate subject. He was then hardly more than a boy in some respects, as indeed I was, too. It was only in later years, when he moved more widely in society, that he understood the bond that could be formed between a man and his mistress and did not shrink from enquiring about such subjects when it was necessary.

I think the professor noticed his hesitation and understood. 'I can have a word with them, or I can ask Mrs Shem to speak to them on the quiet.'

'Thank you,' said Holmes. 'It is vital to know if anyone observed him in those two hours from you last seeing him to the body being discovered. Any small piece of information, however unimportant it might appear, could prove to be most valuable. Did no-one see Summers in the corridor, going from his own room to that of Jones?'

'No. The other men who are staying here were in the gymnasium and never saw Summers that afternoon at all. I can vouch for them. The inspector is going to speak to them, but I don't think he will learn anything.'

'But Summers must have walked there, and taken the carving from its usual place,' mused Holmes. 'What secret reason could he have had for doing so?'

'I only know that he was one of the men who found it unnerved him. I can't imagine why he would even want to touch it.'

'We may know more when the cause of death has been determined,' said Holmes. 'I will ensure that you are kept informed. Does Jones have any family in London?'

'No, his father has been notified of the arrest by telegram and will come up to visit him. And he will engage a legal man to advise him.'

'When I examined Summers's room, I saw a spent fire in the grate, kindling wood and paper, coal in the scuttle, and a small fragment of wood chip, which I believe to be from a matchbox. But I saw no matches. It is a small thing, but it aroused my curiosity.'

'There's a skivvy who comes in each morning, cleans all the grates and lights the fires, and sees to the kitchen stoves,' said Logan. 'The matches are kept in the kitchen and taken back there after use. We don't like the men to smoke in their rooms. We once had one fall asleep in bed with his pipe in his mouth, which didn't do any good to the bedclothes or to him, either. They can smoke in the bar if they so wish.'

'Was Summers a smoker?'

'I never saw him smoke.'

Inspector Sturridge came in just then, and seeing we were still there, gave us a look which strongly suggested he wanted us gone. We decided to take our leave, promising Logan that once the police had departed, we would return. Before we left, Holmes took our glasses back to the counter and handed them to Shem for his attention.

Holmes was lost in thought as we walked away, but he had a familiar spark in his eye. I sometimes imagined it was the outward sign of the great energy blazing in his brain like a fire as it worked on a mystery.

CHAPTER ELEVEN

Later that day over a simple supper in my rooms, I recalled the leaflet given to me by the Furies, one of whom I now knew to be the widow of Matthew Arroway. From Mrs Shem's comments, it was easy to assume that the other two were Mrs Arroway's sister Miss Mitchell and their friend, doctor's wife Mrs Goode. The composition took the form of a printed letter to the public and was composed in a similar impassioned style to that of the widow's appeal in *The Times*. Boxing, she maintained, was an activity which could only debase and brutalise its participants, while attracting thieves and villains to the mob surrounding the ring. She stridently denounced the pugilist whose fists had injured her husband and urged that he be arrested forthwith and charged with murder. She made the valid point that for the crime of murder a case could be brought against the guilty, no matter how much time had passed since the offence. I rather suspected that Mrs Arroway had intended to broadcast the name of the culprit, but it seemed probable that the printer, mindful of the laws of libel, had chosen to omit certain details. Mr Lunn, wherever he might be, remained an innocent man until a jury had declared him guilty and might object to being publicly named. While careful not to spell out the name, therefore, readers had been provided with a clue from which they could make their own deduction: 'L - - - n'.

I showed the paper to Holmes when I next looked in on him in the chemistry laboratory at Barts, where he was creating an assembly of retorts, test tubes, and flasks for his next experiment.

'Have you read this publication?' I asked.

He produced a copy from his pocket. 'I have, and it includes a most serious allegation.'

'No wonder Lunn has disappeared,' I said. 'I think the Furies would descend on him if they knew where he was.'

'If they thought he was the guilty man,' said Holmes.

'Mrs Shem said he was.'

'Have you not noticed the printer's substitution of part of the name? I suggest you look again.'

I hadn't examined it in detail, but now I did and saw what Holmes had noticed. 'There is an extra dash mark in the middle,' I said. 'There ought to be two, as Lunn has only four letters.'

'Logan has five,' observed Holmes.

'But — no, that must be a mistake.'

'I don't believe so. Notice that the paper demands that the murderer be arrested and charged without delay. It does not suggest that there might be any difficulty in locating him, which there would be if the suspect was Mr Lunn.'

I saw his point, which was rather shocking. 'But the professor was not in London then, and his brother doesn't box,' I said.

'We have no proof yet of the first point, although I agree on the second. I took the opportunity yesterday to look closely at Shem Logan's face, especially the nose, ears, and brows. There are very few boxers who do not show some marks of their profession, the great Jem Mace is unusual in that respect, but I am now quite sure that Shem Logan is no Jem Mace and never was. Recall, however, that Mrs Shem said the Arroway fight happened before she was married, before the Logans had the King Henry. This means that all she has told us is what they have told her. It remains possible that Professor Logan was the man and is making sure to claim that he was not present, blaming the incident on an inebriate who cannot be found.' Holmes rubbed his jaw. 'I can certainly attest to the fact that Professor Logan has both the skill and the power to fell a man with one well-directed blow. And since the event was unlawfully conducted, no-one is willing to step forward and tell the truth. Shem Logan, being an employee of the Two Spires, and doing only what he was told to do by the landlord, must be absolved of any complicity in an illegal fight, but of course he supports his brother's innocence. You noticed, did you not, that when the professor spoke to us of the Arroway fight, he failed to mention that his own brother had been there to see it? A notable omission. I rather think that like Mrs Shem, he did not want us to question him, although possibly for a quite different reason.'

I was considering this alarming development, when Surgeon Stevens, who was completing his examination of the body of Bowman, came to see us. 'Here, Holmes, Stamford, as you have an interest in this case, you might like to take a look at this.' He was carrying a crumpled paper bag from which he drew a small brown glass medicine bottle. 'Mrs Bowman has brought this in for me to see. It's a tonic popular with the boxing profession. I don't think it played any part in his death — in fact, I have no doubts that the cause was natural disease — but it might be useful to know more about it before I submit my final report. I'd like to know the formulation, and whether there is any possibility of contamination.'

The bottle was a six-ounce capacity and it bore a printed label: *Dr Wrothby's Strengthening Syrup. A general tonic for the system. Improves athletic performance, works on the large muscles of the body and the heart. Dose one or two teaspoons daily.*

Holmes held the bottle up to the light. 'About four ounces remaining. Did Mrs Bowman say how long he had had this and what dose he took?'

'About one teaspoon a day, but two if he was training for a fight. He had had this bottle for just over a week, she thinks.'

'And it is commonly sold in chemists' shops?'

'Yes. It has been available for quite a number of years.'

'Do we know if Summers also used this tonic? I saw no bottles amongst his effects. The police did make a search of the dustbins, but I don't know if they discovered anything. Really, if they only permitted me to look, they would find so much more. They have already missed several important clues in that case.'

Stevens raised his eyebrows at Holmes's imperious tone but did not ask the obvious question. Those of more senior status who were not acquainted with his brilliance rarely chose to pursue his pronouncements. 'I don't know about Summers,' said Stevens, 'but I will be assisting in his examination. We're being very cautious about prising that idol from his grasp, given the police surgeon's warning, and we won't be able to open the body until we have.'

'I should like to see the carving when it is available,' said Holmes.

It was not a request but a demand, and Stevens hesitated before replying. 'In view of the police surgeon's report, it is intended that the carving, when we have it free, will be carefully sealed, and submitted to Professor Russell together with the stomach contents and samples of viscera and other bodily fluids.' Holmes grunted in disappointment but was obliged to accept the priority granted to the medical college's principal lecturer in chemistry. 'We do have to consider tetanus,' Stevens went on. 'The signs of lockjaw are all there, and we'll be looking closely for a break in the skin and any history of recent injury which might prove to be the cause, but in my opinion, poison is a real possibility.'

'In the meantime, I will busy myself with this mixture.' Holmes uncorked the bottle and essayed a cautious sniff, widening his sensitive nostrils as if appreciating the aroma of a fine wine. 'A bitter preparation, but I think I can guess what line to take.'

Stevens left us to the work.

'If I am not mistaken,' said Holmes, 'this is a common kind of compound tonic, widely used by sportsmen, invalids, and the elderly. It is sold under different names and in a variety of strengths, and principally includes as the active ingredients the phosphates of iron, quinine, and strychnine. Each is valuable to the system on its own, and they are believed to fortify each other in combination. The mixture calms fevers, improves the nerves and the blood, revives a flagging appetite, settles digestion, and, most important to the athlete, maintains bodily strength. Or so the purveyors of such syrups like to claim.'

'I doubt that Bowman was poisoned,' I said. 'He did not exhibit any signs of it.'

'I have made some study of poisons, and I believe that any symptoms from an excess of these ingredients might have taken some while to appear,' said Holmes. 'If, however, the mixture was correctly formulated and Bowman only took the recommended dose, he would not have come to any harm. But let us go to work and satisfy ourselves that Dr Wrothby's preparation is innocent.'

Thinking about Sturridge's theory that the ebony idol had been smeared with poison, I asked, 'Are there poisons that can act through the skin without being ingested?'

'There are, nicotine for example, although it is hard to disguise due to its characteristic scent. I certainly did not detect it on my examination.'

We rolled back our cuffs and made a start. Holmes, it must be said, was a fine chemist. I have worked with him on many occasions, and it was always a pleasure and an education to assist him. His methods might have appeared to be flamboyant, even a little risky, but his determination and insight were extraordinary. In his long career he made many valuable discoveries, leading to advancements in science which ought, when they were considered together, have earned him a knighthood. Holmes, however, had no ambition to secure such accolades. Apart from a few monographs, he usually neglected to claim any credit for his work, which appeared later in the publications of other men.

Our labours complete, we were able to inform Mr Stevens that Dr Wrothby's preparation was the commonplace tonic mixture as Holmes had suspected. The readers of this memoir will no doubt be familiar with a similar and rather more celebrated version of a tonic mixture, sold under the name of Easton's Syrup. None of the active ingredients were present in a proportion that might have given cause for concern. Although the label warned the purchaser not to exceed the stated dose, Holmes estimated that a man of Bowman's weight could have taken six or even eight teaspoons of Dr Wrothby's syrup without experiencing any significant discomfort. Stevens, from his examination, was confident that no more than the usual dose had been taken.

Holmes was undoubtedly frustrated by not being permitted a first look at the idol once it had been extracted from the dead man's grasp. It did not surprise me, therefore, when he later informed me that he had sought and obtained permission to act as an assistant to Professor Russell when he examined the samples taken from poor Summers.

We were finishing our work and about to go our separate ways when Stevens looked in on us again. 'Ah, Holmes, I'm glad I have found you still here. This is a little strange, but there is what I can only describe as a deputation of three ladies asking to speak to you. They say it is very important indeed but will say nothing on the subject to me; however, they did ask for you by name. Respectable-looking. One of them is called Mrs Arroway. She thought you might be able to guess why they wish to consult you.'

'The Furies!' I gasped, before I could stop myself.

Stevens blinked in surprise at my outburst. 'Well, they certainly appeared rather annoyed.'

Holmes smiled. 'I will see them now,' he said.

CHAPTER TWELVE

The three ladies were waiting for us in the visitors' room. They were seated in a row but rose as one body when we entered and faced us together, shoulder to shoulder, like the front line of an army. These were ladies who had become used to opposition and even battle of a sort, and they were prepared to confront their enemies without fear.

'Good afternoon, ladies,' said Holmes, mildly. 'I am Sherlock Holmes, and this is my associate Mr Stamford, who is a medical student. How might we assist you?'

There was a moment's hesitation about my presence, but our visitors quickly glanced at each other, and no objections were raised. 'We must introduce ourselves,' said one of the ladies, stepping forward. She was not unhandsome but might easily have sat for a moving portrait in oils entitled The Careworn Widow. The lines of suffering on her face marked her for about forty years of age, but I suspected she was younger. 'I am the widow of Matthew Arroway, who passed away recently after years of ill health following a boxing match in which his brain was injured.'

'You have suffered greatly,' said Holmes, solicitously. 'I wish to extend my deepest sympathy. I have read your letter to *The Times* and the paper you have distributed. They were extremely moving, and I heartily approve your sentiments.'

Mrs Arroway almost blushed as she acknowledged his reply, and I uttered silent thanks that Holmes had never been tempted to a life of crime, or he would have made a fortune from the practice of deceit.

'This is my sister, Miss Mitchell,' said the widow.

Miss Mitchell was younger than her sister, and stronger looking. I thought it would take more than work and hardship to crush her proud stance and soften her accusing stare, and a great effort to earn her trust. I wondered how she might appear if she was not frowning, but thought I was unlikely to discover that very soon. She uttered a curt greeting.

'And this,' continued Mrs Arroway, 'is our friend Mrs Goode, who has been so very kind to us. Mrs Goode's husband is an eminent doctor.'

Mrs Goode, dressed for the dignity of her position, was a tall lady in her forties. She was making an effort at composure, but only appeared impatient. 'We would like answers to our questions,' she said. 'The police do not assist us. When we learned of the terrible death of Mr Bowman and found that no arrest had been made, I knew it was my duty to report it as a crime, which I did, but all the officer would say was that he had noted my complaint. When I demanded to know what the police would do about it, he either could not or would not tell me. They seem to think these matters do not concern us. We beg to differ. There has been a crime committed, of that there is no doubt. But the greater question, in our opinion, is the continuation of a dangerous activity in the name of sport. We wish to put a stop to it before more men die and more families are plunged into poverty.'

'And you have come to consult me?' asked Holmes, mystified.

Mrs Goode looked a little awkward before she replied. 'As the police turned me away, one of them said to another in a low voice which I believe I was not meant to overhear, that a Mr Holmes of Barts was looking into it, so I sought you out. I thought you might be the man examining the body. I was expecting someone —' She paused.

'More senior?'

'I suppose so. Older, certainly,' she added in an unflattering tone. 'Can you explain your interest in the case?'

Holmes was not discomfited by Mrs Goode's assessment of his position. He rather liked it when people underestimated him, which they did only briefly, and then he had the pleasure of astonishing them. 'I have a penchant for solving mysteries,' he said airily. 'I often provide the police with little observations on their cases which they have missed. I study anatomy and chemistry here, and I also engage in harmless and healthful exercise such as fencing and sparring, so I am familiar with the sporting world. Both Stamford and I were present at the demonstration following which John Bowman died, and Stamford rendered medical assistance. While I cannot anticipate the verdict of the inquest, I do know that evidence will be presented to show that Bowman suffered from a natural disease which no doctor could have diagnosed before he entered the ring, and which resulted in his fatal collapse.'

'Are you saying that boxing was not the cause?' demanded Miss Mitchell.

'That appears to be the case.'

The ladies looked concerned, since an essential plank of their argument was about to be swept away.

'Is it really being claimed that he was deadly ill and showed no sign of it?' said Mrs Goode. 'I find that hard to believe. Such a young man to die so swiftly, it is very rare.'

'His widow informed us that he had symptoms the day before which he thought were those of a cold,' I said. 'The only medicine he was taking was Dr Wrothby's tonic, which many athletes use.'

'Oh, that horrid man!' exclaimed Mrs Arroway with a sudden burst of emotion. 'He was a charlatan, a deceiver! How many deaths could be laid at his door, I wonder?'

'You were acquainted with him?' asked Holmes.

'Yes, after Matthew was hurt, he came to see him. I didn't call him, he just appeared. He visited several times. Oh, he was so kind to us with his comforting words and medicines, and he never took a penny for his trouble, which of course I appreciated, as I had nothing to give him.' She shook her head and took a deep breath before she went on. 'He told me that he had witnessed what happened to my poor husband and was most emphatic that it was an accident, that Matthew had simply slipped and fallen and hit his head. Of course, since he was a doctor, I believed him. There was a time when I would not have listened to a word against Dr Wrothby. When I heard the rumour that he had died, I was terribly upset. I went to his surgery to see if it was true, but it was all locked up. Then I remembered he had once said he looked after the boxers at the King Henry. I actually went there to ask after him, but when I found the place I didn't dare go in. I just stood outside and cried.' She was briefly shaken by the memory, and her sister looked at her carefully. She steadied herself, and with a nod of reassurance, continued.

'Mrs Shem Logan, bless her heart, she is a kindly soul. On learning of my distress, she came out to see what the matter was, and took me into the kitchen and sat me down and made us some tea. She doesn't hold with boxing either. That was when I found out that all that time, Dr Wrothby had lied to me about Matthew, that it was no accident. In fact, over the years he has saved many a man from prosecution by hiding the truth about the dreadful things done in the name of profit. And he was well compensated for it, too. To my mind, he was as much to blame for Matthew's death as anyone else. He only called on us to make sure that I believed his lies and made no fuss about what had happened. He should have put a stop to the fight. The other man was drunk. A wild beast. Unfit. Any doctor worth the name would have seen it. Dr Wrothby must have seen it. He knew. But he let it go on. And who knows what he puts in that so-called tonic. How many men has he poisoned with it?'

CHAPTER THIRTEEN

'This tonic, did he devise and mix it himself?' asked Holmes.

'I would say,' interrupted Mrs Goode, 'that in common with other doctors who advance their own remedies, he might have done so when it was first offered for sale, but in recent years he did no more than give his name to it. There are many similar preparations.' She turned to Mrs Arroway. 'There is no harm in them, really there is not. In fact, they stimulate the heart.' The widow remained angrily unconvinced. 'But I have another question for you, Mr Holmes. As I have said, the purpose of my visit to the police was to ensure that the death of Mr Bowman was treated as a crime. When I mentioned the death of a boxer, however, the policeman thought I meant another case, one not yet in the newspapers — that of a young man who had expired at the King Henry Tavern. That establishment is notorious as a refuge of the boxing fraternity. Once the mistake was established, the policeman realised that he had said too much and would say no more on the subject. Tell me, is it true? I have looked at this morning's papers, but all they say is that a fatal incident occurred. Has there been another boxing death? If so, that is very shocking, and the police really ought to do something.'

Holmes paused before he replied, and I guessed that he was deciding what he might safely reveal. In difficult cases, the police often keep the details very close, in order to better appreciate which witnesses were being truthful, and leave traps open to snare the guilty. Bowman's death had been a very public affair, with newspapermen present at the ringside, but there had been meagre pickings for the press over Summers, and the police would have wanted that to remain so until the inquest. 'There has been another death, yes,' he said, 'and the deceased was a boxer lodging at the King Henry, but it did not take place during a match. His body has been brought here for examination, and I will be assisting a distinguished professor in his work. The inquest will open here tomorrow morning at ten o'clock, although it will only be a formality pending a full report. The inquest on Mr Bowman, however, may well be concluded at the same sitting tomorrow, and if you wish to attend you will hear the evidence for yourself.'

Mrs Arroway's expression suggested that she did not care to listen to the proceedings, and she looked appealingly at Mrs Goode, who smiled and patted her friend's arm. 'I will attend on behalf of us all,' she said. 'The wife of a doctor hears many tales of woe and needs a strong stomach. But even if this other man was not actually boxing at the time of his death, that does not of course absolve the practice of boxing of any blame. Perhaps if he had taken a strengthening tonic, he might be alive today. I assume he did not?'

'Not as far as I am presently aware,' said Holmes. 'All the circumstances will be investigated most diligently, and we may learn that in time.'

'Is there no theory as to cause of death?' said Mrs Arroway.

'Very many,' said Holmes. 'It would be wrong to venture on any speculation at this point.'

'Two young boxers dead within days of each other,' said Miss Mitchell, grimly. 'Three in a few months, if we include Matthew. Something is wrong, and there are men responsible who should be brought to justice. I for one will not be satisfied until that den of iniquity the King Henry is closed down.'

'Yes,' sighed Mrs Arroway. 'Apart from Mrs Shem, who cannot help herself as she is the wife of the manager, they are all in it together. Drinking, gambling, fighting and loose behaviour. No decent woman should patronise that place.'

Mrs Goode nodded. 'I am not of the temperance persuasion myself. Alcoholic beverages do have a place in the medicine cabinet, and a little good wine with dinner aids the digestion, but in excess they stimulate the baser instincts and should be avoided.'

'The man I would like to get my hands on,' said Miss Mitchell, clenching her fists, which were quite impressive, 'is that creature who killed my brother-in-law. If I could find the proof, I would make him confess, take him by the collar and drag him to the police.'

'And this person is?' asked Holmes.

There were a few moments of consideration. 'Mrs Shem told me his name was Lunn,' said Mrs Arroway, at last, 'but we are wondering if she has been misled, perhaps deliberately. We have heard another rumour, but we can't prove it, that the man who killed my husband was none other than Professor Logan, the licensee of the King Henry, who thrives off his reputation as a boxer and has become rich from spilling the blood of others.'

'Of course, we dare not state or publish explicitly which of these two men we suspect, or the law would not approve,' said Mrs Goode, quickly. 'Worse still, neither would my husband.'

'We must be careful,' agreed Mrs Arroway.

Miss Mitchell did not look inclined to be careful. 'If you like to find the answers to mysteries, Mr Holmes, then here is another one for you. Prove who it was who committed this outrage, either Lunn or Logan or another man, whoever he might be, and bring him to justice.'

'On what day did Mr Arroway suffer his injury?' asked Holmes.

'It was Wednesday 8th March 1871,' said the widow, pressing her hand to her heart as if she could feel that date forever engraved there.

Holmes wrote this information in his notebook. 'I accept the challenge,' he said with a disarming bow.

The three ladies, who appeared unused to getting their own way quite so easily, drew aside for a brief consultation. Mrs Arroway then thanked Holmes for his promise of help, wished him success in his endeavour, and asked to be informed of any progress.

'I will make sure to do so. I ask only that if you are to discover anything further that might assist my enquiries, you will communicate it to me immediately,' said Holmes.

'We will notify you at once,' said Mrs Goode. Our business was now done to the satisfaction of all, and the ladies made their departure.

I was a little concerned at the extent of Holmes's ambition in this curious case. 'That will be a difficult case to solve. The match must have been made secretly, and I doubt that any of the company would admit to being there. How do you hope to find the answers?'

'By keeping my eyes open, learning all the facts and taking nothing at face value,' said Holmes. 'That was a curiously interesting visit,' he added thoughtfully. 'Did you not observe anything remarkable about the ladies?'

'I — well — they seemed very determined. And I wouldn't wager on any man's chances if Miss Mitchell ever got hold of him.'

'It was their questions. Not merely a matter of what questions they asked, but what questions they did not ask. They are anxious to seek the truth, but as is so often the case, there may be truths already in their possession they would rather not reveal.' And that was all he would say on that subject for the present. 'And now, I anticipate that for several days to come, my time will be thoroughly occupied with assisting Professor Russell, in which case, Stamford, I need to engage your help.'

'What do you wish me to do?' I found myself saying.

'I would like you to discover as much as you can about Dr Wrothby.'

CHAPTER FOURTEEN

This did not on first view, appear to be a dangerous task. I really ought to have been more alert.

'If the accusations against him are true,' Holmes went on, 'then he was engaged over many years in being complicit in criminal behaviour, and even acting as an accessory to manslaughter and murder, by concealing unlawfully conducted boxing matches from the police.'

'But he is beyond the reach of the law, now,' I observed.

'He is, but there might be associates who are not, and who are still busy making mischief in the world of boxing. Knowing his history could lead me to them. Boxing, if conducted properly, is a noble sport and I would not see it besmirched with disrepute or even banned altogether because of the actions of a few.'

There was no arguing with that statement, and I naturally agreed to see what I could do. I was as eager as Holmes not to be late for the forthcoming inquest, so I arrived at Barts early the following morning to consult the archives. Fortunately, the hospital records were well kept, and I was quickly able to establish that there was nothing in them relating to Dr Wrothby. He had not studied at Barts, was never employed there, and neither had he been the subject of a post-mortem examination or inquest at Barts. I was about to admit defeat and report my failure to Holmes when the keeper of the archives asked me about the subject of my research. 'Just wait a moment,' he said. 'I might have something for you.'

It transpired that there was an informal collection of newspaper cuttings taken from the journals supplied to the students' reading room, relating to notable medical issues, including trials and inquests. The archivist even maintained a useful index of names, and Wrothby's was amongst them. I settled down to what I hoped would be an interesting hour or so.

Obituaries, letters to the newspapers from Wrothby's friends, and others not so kindly disposed, who preferred to remain anonymous, and the proceedings of the doctor's inquest provided me with a picture of the man's life and his strange and lonely death.

Dr Wrothby was aged fifty-five when he died. He had had a medical practice with a surgery at his home in one of the less fashionable parts of West London for many years and was a familiar sight as he made his rounds in a dilapidated chaise drawn by an elderly but biddable horse. His medical knowledge and treatment had never been called into question, but he was known to make merry with more alcohol than was good for him once his rounds were over, and some patients had even complained about the smell of beer on his breath when they consulted him next morning. His regular practice was small and dwindling, but his main activity was attending to the injuries and general requirements of pugilists.

One cold night in February 1873 he had been drinking liberally at the King Henry, which was his regular haunt. Having taken even more than was usual for him, he had thrown off his customary merriment, and descended into a maudlin frame of mind in which he reminisced about the past and those persons he had known who were now deceased. The landlord, Professor Logan, suggested that it was high time for him to return home to his wife, and guided him carefully but firmly to the door which led to the coachyard, where his horse was waiting patiently. The last person to see Dr Wrothby alive was one of the barmaids, Annie, who was disposing of some waste in the dustbin and saw him in his chaise, driving out of the yard into the main street.

Mrs Wrothby usually waited up for her husband's return, but that night she was suffering from a chill. Assuming he would not be home until late, she dismissed the servant and retired to her bed. On waking the next morning, she discovered that her husband was not at home. She decided to go and look for him, but on leaving the house found him in the nearby stable yard, sitting in the chaise, still grasping the reins in his hands. He was cold and quite dead. She summoned the servant, who helped her carry the corpse indoors and lay it out as well as could be done, for *rigor mortis* was well established, and the body had stiffened in the seated position. The servant was sent to summon a doctor. He was Jedediah Goode, M.D., who pronounced Dr Wrothby dead and agreed to officiate at the post-mortem examination, which took place as soon as it became possible, at the house.

A large attendance was expected at the inquest, which was held in the large upstairs gymnasium room of the King Henry Tavern, before a substantial crowd of the boxing fraternity. Mrs Wrothby, thickly veiled and stricken with grief, was one of the principal witnesses. Weeping, she said she could not help but wonder if she had not retired to bed early that night, and had therefore discovered her husband when he first arrived home and brought him indoors, he might still be alive. The servant, a self-possessed young female of about fourteen, called Sally, confirmed her mistress's account. That evening, Mrs Wrothby, commenting that the master was not yet returned, and complaining of having to wait up for him when the weather was so bad, had sent her to bed, and retired for the night. She had observed nothing further until being awoken the following morning to assist her mistress in carrying the corpse indoors. She had then run to fetch the nearest doctor.

A neighbour testified that on hearing Mrs Wrothby call for assistance she had gone to help, and while the body was being carried indoors she had volunteered to look after the horse, which was in a very bedraggled state having been out all night. She was surprised, given the age and neglect of this animal, that it had not expired too, after being in the cold and untended for so long. It was not fit for anything and had been sold to a knacker soon afterwards.

Several persons from the King Henry, where Dr Wrothby had spent his last evening, told the court that his attendance had not been marked by any disagreements, or quarrels, either verbal or violent. Dr Wrothby had been in an unusually melancholy frame of mind, musing on the past and those he had known who had gone to their rest. He had occasionally been seen in a similar state but was always recovered the next day and with hardly any memory of the night before.

Dr Goode testified that in view of the advancement of *rigor*, he estimated that Dr Wrothby had died some hours before he was found. *Livor mortis*, staining from the settling of the blood after death, showed that he had died where he sat, in the chaise. On examining the body, he had found a great number of bruises, some of them several days old, although one slight mark on the temple was quite fresh. However, he had been informed by Mrs Wrothby that her husband, when inebriated, often bumped into the furniture or walls, and he bruised very easily. Dr Goode did not consider the bruises to be of any importance in the death. Excessive frequent drinking did often lead to superficial bruising of that nature. He had seen similar appearances on the bodies of other inebriates. He concluded that Dr Wrothby had died from exposure to the cold, a condition made more serious and rapid in its effect by his prodigious and inadvisable consumption of alcohol. The heart and respiration had simply stopped. He thought it was quite possible that the condition of the deceased had been too advanced to be recovered soon after the chaise drew to a halt, and he had slipped into unconsciousness and died soon afterwards. Dr Goode attached no blame whatsoever to Mrs Wrothby.

The inquest jury was not faced with a difficult decision and returned a verdict of death by misadventure. The foreman said they also wished to place on record a warning to the public against the dangers of drink, a sentiment wholly approved of by the coroner, who said that too many persons died before their time as a result of that pernicious habit.

I was able to complete my notes in time to appear at the Barts stewards' office, where that morning's inquests were to commence.

CHAPTER FIFTEEN

The gathering was a small one, and the number of live bodies did little to help the meagre fire warm the room. Mrs Goode arrived on the hour, doing her best not to attract special notice. Anyone who observed her would have assumed that she was a grieving family member relating to one of the cases being heard. She sat quietly, her face concealed by a veil, but the position of her head and attitude of her shoulders suggested intent observation. There was a woman present in widow's weeds being comforted by another lady, also in mourning, and we assumed this was Mrs Bowman and a relative. Professor Logan arrived, top hatted and wearing a greatcoat with a fur collar. He still resembled a pirate, but one who had found a chest of gold and wanted to appear as a gentleman.

When Holmes appeared, in a cloud of chemical fragrance, I passed him the fruits of my labours. He quickly perused them while waiting for the proceedings to start.

Two strangers arrived, in formal attire, one of whom we were sure must be the father of Jim Jones, and the other, who was clutching a leather document case, his legal advisor. They sat together, occasionally conferring in whispers.

The session opened without any surprises. The inquest on Bowman was soon concluded. I gave my observations as the first medical man to attend him, followed by Dr Ridgeway, who made short work of his testimony and hurried away without waiting to hear the verdict.

The coroner decided to spare the widow the pain of testifying and called Surgeon Stevens to give the principal evidence. Stevens, in clear unambiguous terms, stated that the boxer had died from an embolism in the lungs. The physical activity of the sparring demonstration might have caused the separation of the large blood clot that had formed in his leg, but he believed that this might have occurred at any time, during normal exercise or even walking in the street. The event could not have been predicted, and the other boxer was not to blame. The jury, directed by the coroner, had no hesitation in bringing a verdict of death by natural causes.

Mrs Bowman, supported by her friend, rose and departed. I glanced at Mrs Goode to see if the verdict had been a disappointment, but there was no dip of the head or slump of the shoulders; she remained immobile. The coroner opened the inquest on Bill Summers.

The jury had viewed the body, which, so Holmes informed me, had finally been persuaded to give up its grip on the idol, while the features had relaxed into a more natural expression.

The only witness was a sturdy man in his fifties with scarred eyebrows, called Harry Baxter. He was a long-retired pugilist who had set himself up as a 'matchmaker' for good prospects in the boxing ring. He had had the dreadful task of formally identifying the body of his best man, Bill Summers, whom he believed was aged twenty-four. There were tears in his eyes as he told the court that he had first noticed young Summers two years previously, carrying boxes of fruit and vegetables in a street market, and he had instantly seen the youth's potential. He had arranged for him to train with a professional, and after a number of well-received matches in his native Norfolk, he had brought him to London where a more lucrative career beckoned. Baxter had been happy to have Summers lodge and train with his old friend Calum Logan at the King Henry. On the day of the young boxer's death, he had been at a club in Shoreditch, arranging a match for another prospect, and had only learned of the tragedy when he came to the King Henry later that night. As far as he knew, Summers was an orphan.

Baxter was asked to remain in London until the surgeon's report was presented, as he might be questioned further, and he said he would, as he had further business to conduct in the capital. He could be found at the King Henry in the next week if needed or would provide an address if elsewhere thereafter. He was allowed to stand down. The inquest on Summers was adjourned for a week. When we glanced around, Mrs Goode had left the room, and Baxter, too, had departed, looking like a man who had money to make.

The professor came to speak to us and introduced us to Mr Jones senior and his lawman, a Mr Stockdale. They were of a similar age, about fifty years. I realised that Holmes and I must both look terribly young to be of any use in the case, but as he so often did, Holmes managed by his manner and bearing to impress the two gentlemen. Stockdale handed us a sheet of headed notepaper with the address of their London hotel in case we needed to see them. He told us that young Jones had been questioned at length by the police, and repeatedly invited to confess to the murder of Summers, but he had held firm. Inspector Sturridge had then made strenuous efforts to discover something with which he could charge him so as to keep him in custody, but he had failed. Jones had been released, but with a warning not to leave London and was required to provide an address where he could be found. His father had already reserved a room for him at the hotel, where he was now lodged, and his effects had been removed from the King Henry and brought to him there. The carving, which was still being investigated, remained at Barts.

Once the visitors had taken their leave, the professor confided that he had offered accommodation to them gratis at the King Henry, but Mr Stockdale had advised against it, saying he would not put it past Inspector Sturridge to look for signs of their having influenced witnesses.

The question of Summers's death remained open and would do so until the inquest reached a verdict. It was feared that any question of Jones's involvement would not be settled until there was irrefutable proof of his innocence, proof which would almost certainly involve the conviction of another man.

Holmes had had no time to commence his enquiries into the whereabouts of the boxer, Lunn, who was still, to his mind, the most likely culprit in the death of Matthew Arroway. He now addressed the professor. 'Once my work on the Summers case is complete, I would like, if I may, to speak to your brother about the events leading to the death of Matthew Arroway,' he said. 'I am aware that he is the only man still living who has admitted to seeing that fight. Would he be willing to tell me what he knows?'

The professor, who if he recalled that he had omitted his brother's involvement from his own account, was unabashed at Holmes's words, shook his head. 'He won't talk of it nowadays,' he said. 'Mrs Shem has spoken to me and said that she has told you all she can. I shouldn't think there is anything else to learn. What is your interest in that affair, Holmes? It can't have anything to do with Summers.'

'As you know, I like to pursue unsolved mysteries when they cross my path,' said Holmes. 'Let us put it down to natural curiosity.'

'If you must,' said Logan with a shrug.

'Did you ever fight Lunn?' asked Holmes. 'Did you know his quality?'

The professor grinned. 'I did, some years before his fight with Arroway, and took a good beating for my trouble. We were well matched, but I learned a profitable lesson that day. If you can escape one fist easily, watch out for the other one. His left hook was weaker, but he knew how to use it, and then his right did the damage. That is the trick I caught you with.'

'Are there any portraits of Lunn in the sporting press?'

'I have never seen one.'

'Describe him.'

'Well, he was a good size. Taller than me, almost your height, but broad with it, a good solid weight.' He flexed his jaw, thoughtfully. 'Got a lot of power behind the punch.'

'Any other details that might identify him would be useful,' said Holmes, his tone suggesting that he was disinclined to identify his quarry by inviting likely individuals to punch him. 'The colour of his hair?'

'Hmm, can't say I noticed his hair. Light rather than dark, I suppose.'

'Any noticeable scars or marks?'

'Nothing out of the ordinary. And I don't know the colour of his eyes, either, before you ask,' he added with a chuckle. 'But here's the thing: the last time we talked about Lunn, I said I heard he had gone to America, but when I thought about it, I realised that it was just a rumour. No-one actually saw him go. Now, I always keep an eye out for all the boxing news both here and in America, and since Lunn fought Arroway, I have never heard any news of him at all.'

'Is he a married man?' asked Holmes.

'No, I believe he lived with a widowed sister. And I don't know her name or address.'

Holmes's expression had hardened as he headed back to his work, and I sensed a fresh determination to uncover the mystery of the fate of the elusive Mr Lunn.

CHAPTER SIXTEEN

'You will have to extend my apologies to Professor Logan,' said Holmes next morning. 'I was hoping to attend the gymnasium for a lesson this afternoon, but it now appears that I will be engaged in the laboratory all day in the case of Summers. I will advise him when I have some information which I am permitted to disclose.'

I was due for another sparring class, and on my arrival at the King Henry on a dull and windy afternoon, I found the professor, Walter Robson and Harry Baxter in the gymnasium, and busy classes in progress. Baxter was walking about and appeared to be inspecting the boxers in training as a butcher might size up cattle going to market. He watched me train, but not for long.

When I was done, Logan introduced me to Baxter, and praised me for my efforts in helping Bowman. 'I was pleased to hear the inquest absolve Jones of any fault in Bowman's death,' said Logan, 'and I hope to hear the same about Summers in due course.'

'I saw the body, as you know,' said Baxter, 'and it's my opinion that the poor lad must have died of fright. He was not the timid type — at least, he wasn't afraid of anything living, but he had some unusual ideas and allowed them to upset his mind. When he went for his very first fight, he found a sixpence lying on the pavement and put it in his pocket. He said it was his lucky sixpence and he never went anywhere without it. He was going to have it fastened to a watch chain. But about a week ago, he lost it. There was a hole in his pocket, and it must have dropped through. I've never seen a grown fellow so disconsolate over a sixpence. Then when he heard about Jones and his ebony idol, he said, "That's it, I'm done for!" I tried to reassure him, I told him to put it out of his mind and just make himself as strong as possible, but instead of more training I think he did less. And he was off his food, which was unusual for him.'

'Did he consult a doctor?' I asked.

'No, there was nothing wrong with him, it was all nerves. And a doctor might have told him not to fight, which wouldn't have done at all.'

'Was he going to pull out of the match?'

'He was thinking that way, but I told him he couldn't. There was a signed agreement, and the devil to pay if he simply changed his mind.'

'I have never heard of a healthy man his age dying from fright,' I said.

Baxter, his opinion unshaken, gave me a dubious glance. 'Well, you're young yet. I daresay there's all sorts you don't know.' Robson simply gave a derisive chuckle.

I was invited to accompany the men to the lounge bar for some refreshment. There was a corner where Robson liked to sit in an old worn armchair, and he settled himself in his accustomed place for which he had no rivals. The rest of us gathered about a table, while the professor ordered drinks to be brought. I recognised the barmaid who served us as one of the three I had seen on the evening of Summers's death, looking at her distressed friends in dismay. Her features betrayed no emotion now, but the cheeriness one often associates with barmaids, who like to offer a friendly face to customers, was noticeably absent.

Professor Logan, who had been working hard with his class and had built up a healthy thirst, took only a small glass of beer, along with some cooling water, and I asked for the same. Baxter and Robson, on the other hand, were unafraid to drink deep, which they did in a manner suggesting long practice. The two older men listened intently as Logan questioned me about the work that Holmes was carrying out regarding young Summers, and what causes of death were being considered.

I decided to adopt Holmes's line of response in the case and replied that it was too early to say. Holmes was always careful not to advance too many theories to the uninformed, as they tended to seize upon the most sensational ideas which were always the most memorable, and then declare them to be facts. Once this position had been adopted, even convincing evidence to the contrary often failed to move them.

'I expect you'll be called to give evidence next week,' I told Baxter. 'You must know Summers's habits better than anyone. Was he a drinker?'

'Not that I noticed. And my men are always told not to drink before a match. I am very strict about that. The occasional stimulant doesn't do any harm,' he added, matching the action to the word.

'Did he take medicinal stimulants? Like Dr Wrothby's tonic?'

Baxter wrinkled his nose in disgust. 'I don't encourage that. Clean living, plenty of good food, regular exercise, and liniment. That's what I tell them. In any case, young Summers didn't like those tonics. He tried Wrothby's once and said it was bitter. I tasted it and had to agree. I still think brandy is the best medicine for a flagging boxer.'

This conversation led me to think about Holmes's interest in the late doctor, and what might be the best way of discovering more about him. 'I wonder,' I said, 'do any of you know where Mrs Wrothby might be found? I think Holmes would like to speak with her.'

There was a moment of silence from my companions, before Baxter asked, 'What is his interest?'

I hesitated. 'There have been allegations made against her late husband, which may or may not be true. Mrs Arroway —'

'Oh, that lady, she is very persistent,' said Logan, dismissively.

'Holmes merely wishes to know the truth. This is out of consideration for Mrs Arroway. She is still suffering after her recent widowhood. He might be able to set her mind at rest.'

'I haven't seen Mrs Wrothby for a long time,' said Logan. 'The doctor used to send her round with his liniments, but then he died, and the practice was sold up, and after that she stopped coming.'

'I chanced to see her quite recently,' said a voice, and we looked round and saw Mrs Shem, who had come to collect our empty glasses.

CHAPTER SEVENTEEN

'Mrs Wrothby? Is that so?' said Logan. 'Did you speak to her?'

'No, she was coming out of a tea shop in company with another lady, and I thought she was looking very comfortable and content. I wasn't sure if I ought to greet her, and I might have done, but then she saw me, and I knew from her expression that she preferred not to be recognised. Then she turned her back on me and walked away.'

Professor Logan nodded but made no comment.

'I was glad for her sake that her situation has improved,' added Mrs Shem. 'Wrothby never gave her much of an allowance, and he made her work all hours. Her gowns and shawls were always patched and worn. She is better off with his fortune than his company.'

'Wrothby was a dark horse,' declared Robson, abruptly.

'He was a scoundrel,' said Baxter, 'but he was boxing's scoundrel. I will hear no ill of him.'

'There was good and bad in him,' said Logan. 'We all have reason to be grateful to him, even if he could be hard to manage.' He turned to Robson. 'You know that better than most.'

'I know what I know,' said Robson. He took a large draught from his tankard. 'I can still hear his voice. I can't get rid of it.'

'The drink talked loud with him,' said Baxter.

'That it did,' Logan agreed.

'He still hangs about here, hoping for a drink,' said Robson. 'I've seen him sitting in his old place, in the public bar. He likes to be there with his boxing friends.'

'I didn't know ghosts could drink,' said Baxter with a nervous laugh.

'I have never seen him,' said Mrs Shem, gathering up the glasses. 'And if I do, I will put a drink before him and see what he does with it.'

Baxter chuckled, but the other two men did not.

'If any of you happen to see Mrs Wrothby again,' I said, 'you might venture to speak to her. Holmes would like to know her address. She must have a card. Perhaps he would be permitted to call. Or you could mention that if she came to Barts and asked to speak to Sherlock Holmes at the medical college, then someone could direct her to him.'

I could not help but notice that the convivial atmosphere had gone, and things took a chilly turn. The name of Wrothby was clearly not one anyone present wished to savour. I decided it would be best for me to finish my drink and go. I got my coat and muffler, wished everyone a good night, and took my leave. I walked briskly along the lane, and was passing the entrance to the coach yard, when a figure suddenly loomed up in front of me. It was Walter Robson.

I think I might have exclaimed something like, 'Oh, Mr Robson, you gave me a fright —' and was hoping to move around him so we didn't collide, but I was not afforded the chance. He seized hold of my lapels, pulled me bodily into the narrow alley and pushed me against the wall, where I struck my head smartly on the brickwork. He was not as strong as he had been in his youth, especially in the lower body, but there was no mistaking the power of a seasoned pugilist in his grip. I gasped, which was a bad idea as I took in a lungful of beer and stale tobacco from his panting breath. The yellow light of a nearby gas lamp gave him an evil look, like a pantomime demon. His face was contorted with anger, and close up, I saw it was deeply furrowed and crossed with small scars, his unshaven cheeks covered in grey stubble like the prickles of a sea urchin.

'Now, I don't mean to hurt you, Mr Stamford,' he snarled, which was something of a relief, because his actions rather suggested otherwise, 'but I want you to take a message to your nosey friend. Even if we knew where to find Mrs Wrothby, which we don't, we wouldn't tell him. Because we can guess the real reason he wants to speak to her, and it's nothing to do with that meddling Mrs Arroway, who would be better off put in an asylum. Mrs Wrothby, and we have nothing but respect for that lady, has suffered quite enough and she is the last person who needs to be questioned about her husband. Now, there's those that say that what's past is past and what's done is done, and what with the man being dead and all, you need pay it no mind. But Dr Wrothby has friends, many friends in the world of boxing who go back to the old times. I knew him well in those days, and I can tell you there are those who wouldn't be too pleased about anyone poking and prying. So you just go and tell Mr Holmes that.' He let go of my coat and pushed me again. This time, I was able to brace my arms against the wall behind me to prevent another crack to the head. 'You won't be told twice!'

I gasped out some words of agreement to his wishes, and scampered away before he thought to seize me again, imagining that a horde of thick-knuckled bullies was waiting for me around every corner. Of course, they were not, and Robson made no attempt to pursue me. I am not a courageous battler, but I am extremely adept at running away from danger. Fortunately, I was not badly hurt, and when I arrived home a cold cloth soon brought down the small swelling on my scalp. I did not sleep well that night.

When I next spoke to Holmes, telling him all that had happened, he merely said, 'How very interesting.'

Once I was a little calmer, I began to wonder how much danger Robson actually was to me. He was accustomed to using his fists, but he was nearly three times my age, and I saw in his movement and posture obvious signs of weak legs and back. Nevertheless, if he had really wanted to hurt rather than frighten me, which he had certainly achieved, I felt sure that he was more than capable of doing me a serious injury.

My first instinct following this assault had been not to return to classes at the gymnasium, but then I thought what a poor example of a man I would be if I allowed Robson's threats to keep me away. I imagined his contempt and Holmes's disappointment. My mettle, never of the finest, crawled back, cloaked in shame.

'I have been making my own discoveries about Dr Wrothby,' said Holmes. 'I had been wondering why, given the humble nature of his practice, the man called to the house on the day he died was Dr Jedediah Goode, who has a long-established and substantial practice in Mayfair. How come he was the nearest man to be found? The answer is a simple one. Dr Wrothby's practice was not far distant but in a less fashionable street, and a servant in a hurry might have arrived at Dr Goode's in ten minutes. According to the most recently published directory, Dr Goode is the only doctor of that name with a practice in London, so presumably he is the husband of Mrs Goode, whom we have met. I notice she wears a discreet veil when handing out leaflets with her associates. I am not sure what her husband might have to say about it if he knew she was out in all weathers, creating trouble.'

'Given that Wrothby had largely neglected his regular practice and devoted his attention to ministering to boxers, and the consumption of alcohol, I had been wondering if his widow had discovered him to be bankrupt,' I said. 'But the location of his surgery could make the practice a valuable acquisition for a more active man.'

'Indeed. Mrs Wrothby might have done better than we imagined from the sale. At least, from what you say, she has abandoned her rags and bought herself a new gown. There is another possibility, of course. Dr Wrothby's legacy might have included the proceeds of crime. The question is, how much does she know of his criminal past? There might be information in her possession which could, if exposed, lead others to prison, or even the gallows.'

'You will not abandon your investigation, then, Holmes?'

He smiled. 'I shall pursue it with greater energy than before.'

CHAPTER EIGHTEEN

The following morning, Holmes informed me that he had completed his work for Professor Russell, who had retired to his office to write his report on the death of Bill Summers. Holmes was tight-lipped about the result. 'We have arrived at a conclusion, but Professor Russell has ordered me to say nothing to anyone until the result is made public,' was all he would say. I would not have betrayed any confidences, but it was useless to say so, and I had to be content to respect that decision. 'However, I intend to pay a visit to the former practice of Dr Wrothby to see if there is anything the current incumbent can tell me. Are you busy, Stamford?' he added casually.

I sensed that he required my presence, and so accompanied him, certain that any contribution he required would not add to my glory.

The line between poverty and wealth in London can be a remarkably thin one. We began by confirming the location of Dr Jedediah Goode's medical practice, which enjoyed a substantial reputation. The consulting rooms boasted an elegantly impressive frontage, with, I suspected, fees to match. From there, it wanted only a short walk to the address that had once been Dr Wrothby's. Despite the proximity of the two practices, it was obvious that Wrothby and Goode would not have competed for patients. We found ourselves in a street of terraced properties, most of which were probably lodging houses, outwardly respectable but a little dejected. Narrow cuts led between some of the houses to shared stable yards, for use either by those living in that street or other more prosperous parts beyond, who were able to aspire to a carriage. The house where Dr Wrothby had once practised medicine would surely have once looked like the others, but following his death it must have received the house equivalent of a 'wash and brush up' as it is termed. There was a pair of unnecessarily large urns on either side of the freshly painted front door, clearly a recent improvement, which was furnished with a handsome knocker. Attached to the wall beside it was a brass plate with details of surgery times, and the name of the surgeon: Rbt. Goode.

'Recently qualified, and almost certainly a relation of the distinguished Jedediah,' said Holmes. 'When the doctor was called to inspect the corpse of the late Dr Wrothby, he would also have taken notice of a medical practice which would soon be for sale.' Holmes took a little perambulation about the premises. 'If I read the plate and the carriage tracks correctly, the doctor is out on his rounds.'

The adjoining stable yard, accessible to smaller carriages, was, I reminded myself, the site of Dr Wrothby's death. Holmes took a turn about the enclosure, which was as well swept as might be desired, then he looked up at the house. I followed his gaze. From this position, we were able to see one side of the building. The only window overlooking the yard was little more than an attic skylight. 'It is certainly possible, if Mrs Wrothby had retired to bed early, that she would not have been able to observe her husband's later arrival,' Holmes commented. 'But we shall call next door and see what we can learn there.'

The property beside the surgery had once been a three-storey house, but the ground floor had undergone a transformation into a small shop with bright paint and clean windows. The items on display included tall glass carboys filled with coloured water, porcelain unguent jars and inhalation bottles. There was a large poster stating that Dr Goode's medicinal preparations and pure foodstuffs could be purchased there, and these unrivalled products supplied everything required to ensure the robust health of both adults and children. For the avoidance of further doubt, the sign above the window read: *Jas. Goode, Chemist and Druggist.*

'Another relative,' I said. Holmes did not disagree, and I followed him into the shop.

The interior, which had once been a front parlour, had been fitted out with rows of shelving on all sides, displaying a wide array of bottles, jars and canisters, and there were posters advertising the sale of patent and proprietary remedies and wholesome nourishment suitable for invalids. Given the season, coughs, colds and fevers were a common theme. There is a particular fragrance about chemists' shops which I have always found rather pleasant, an admixture of sweet herbs with a bitter reminder of the less agreeable flavours that lurked beneath the syrups, and the stinging scent of liniments. This one smelt mainly of polish. A young lady with a white linen apron over her gown was behind the counter, handing a neatly wrapped package to a lady customer, and we saw through a window at the rear of the premises a man moving about in the dispensary.

We waited for the customer to depart, and I had the feeling that I was once again to be called upon to act the part of a young gentleman with shaken nerves. That day, the situation was not so far from the truth.

'Good afternoon,' said Holmes to the young lady once we were able to approach the counter. 'As you see, my friend here is in need of a general tonic for the system, and we have heard good things spoken of Dr Wrothby's strengthening syrup. Do you have such an item for sale?'

The young lady smiled. 'We do not stock Wrothby's medicines, but I can recommend something which our customers consider to be even better.' She took a bottle down from a nearby display stand, which bore a legend recommending Dr Goode's medicines, pills, and liniments. 'This is Dr Goode's Superior Strengthening Syrup. It is an excellent general tonic for the blood, the heart and the circulation.'

Holmes took the bottle and made a great play of studying the label. 'In what way is this superior to Dr Wrothby's preparation?' he asked, casually.

'It is both pleasanter to taste, and more effective,' said the young lady, brightly.

I was eager to study the label, which was attractively printed and listed the ingredients in small lettering, but decided to leave that pleasure to Holmes as I was supposed to be a debilitated invalid.

Holmes looked about him. 'Am I right in recalling that Dr Wrothby once had a practice near here? I am sure I heard someone speak of it.'

'Yes, the late Dr Wrothby formerly conducted his practice from the surgery next door. That practice is now conducted by Dr Goode, who is my brother-in-law.'

'Really? Not the noted Jedediah Goode?'

She smiled. 'No, Dr Robert Goode, his son. It is an easy mistake to make, as Robert only came here quite recently.'

'Ah, and am I right in supposing that Mr Goode the chemist is his brother?'

'That is so, yes. Mr James Goode is my husband.'

Holmes did some thoughtful nodding, as if taking time to absorb the information. 'I wonder — would you be so kind as to let me know where Mrs Wrothby resides nowadays?'

The young lady seemed a little taken aback by that request, and Holmes went on, 'My dear mother is a great enthusiast of her husband's tonic, which she likes to say is a cure for all her ills. But I have no doubt that she will find Dr Goode's tonic even better. She was most upset to learn that Dr Wrothby had passed away and thought she would like to pay a visit to the widow, if that would be appreciated.'

'I am sorry, but I do not have an address for Mrs Wrothby,' said the young lady.

'Perhaps your husband can advise me?' said Holmes. He placed the bottle of syrup on the counter and took some coins from his pocket.

No longer cheerful, Mrs James Goode appeared to be on the verge of denying this seemingly innocent request, but then roused her features once more into a smile. 'Of course, I will ask him.'

She tapped on the dispensary window, and a few moments later the chemist appeared. He was hardly more than a year or two older than me but was trying to look more distinguished with an arrangement of the hair and whiskers suitable for a more mature individual. Holmes explained that he would like the address of Mrs Wrothby.

The young chemist glanced at his wife, who gave a small shake of the head, which he then copied. 'I am sorry, but the lady did not leave a forwarding address when she vacated the premises.'

'What a shame,' said Holmes. 'Does she have relations who might know her address?'

'I couldn't say.'

'You have no news of her at all?' asked Holmes.

'None. I really cannot help you.'

Holmes sighed despondently as he paid for the tonic, and the young lady wrapped it in paper. 'Perhaps Mrs Wrothby has left London,' he said, 'or she might have gone to live with a relative. She might even have returned to her maiden name, as some widows do. I must look into that.'

At this last comment, the chemist smiled. 'I think she may well have done so,' he said. 'I am not sure if you are aware of this, but the name Wrothby is chiefly known in boxing circles, which some people find unsavoury. A respectable lady might well wish to divest herself of that name.'

We thanked him and took our leave.

'It is a pity they could tell us nothing,' I said.

'On the contrary,' said Holmes, 'they may have told us more than they realise. But I have work to do, as I am not yet in possession of a number of vital facts.'

Whatever Holmes was planning was interrupted, since the following morning he was urgently summoned back to the laboratory by Professor Russell.

CHAPTER NINETEEN

I was at work in the library that afternoon when one of the students approached me with a look of concern, a look which I was beginning to recognise, as I had seen it so often. He beckoned me outside for a talk, and I could guess what he was about to say. 'Do you know where Holmes is?' he asked.

'He has been assisting Professor Russell,' I said. 'The Summers case, I believe.'

His made a disappointed face. 'I thought as much. He won't want to be disturbed.'

'What is the matter?'

'There is a lady, a very nice, respectable little lady, a Mrs Logan, who has come to see him, and she seems rather upset. She asked for Holmes most particularly and would accept no substitute. Do you know what it is about? Is she a relative?'

'She is not, but I believe I know the general subject of her enquiry. I'll go and speak to her, and I would be obliged if you could advise Holmes that she is here. It may not be possible for him to come and see her straight away, but he ought to know.' The student hurried away to notify Holmes, and I abandoned my studies to go and see Mrs Logan.

As I suspected, the arrival was Mrs Shem. She had been placed in the visitors' room, where I found her pacing the floor, in a flurry of impatience. She whirled around hopefully as I entered, and I saw her face fall when she saw I was not Holmes.

'I am sorry, but Holmes is currently very busy on important work concerning the enquiry on Summers, and I don't know if he can be interrupted,' I said. 'I have sent someone to tell him that you are here. If he can be spared to come and see you, he will, but I can't promise that he can, or that he will be able to tell you anything. But do please tell me what the matter is, and even if I am unable to assist you, I will make sure that he knows.'

Mrs Shem looked a little relieved at this. 'The police came round again this morning,' she said, breathlessly. 'The whole tavern has been closed down, and everyone is being questioned again. I told that inspector that Mr Holmes was looking into it, and I am afraid he was rather brusque. But the sergeant told us before that Mr Holmes has advised the police in the past on scientific matters and that he is trustworthy.'

She sat down, looking suddenly very weary, and I took a seat beside her. I offered her some refreshment, but she shook her head. 'I wasn't expecting this,' she said miserably. 'They made a great many searches when Summers's body was found, and I thought that would be all we had to endure, but when they came back today it was different. They have searched the entire premises. Everything. The bars, the storerooms, the cellars, the kitchen, the pantry, the bedrooms, the gymnasium. They were especially interested in the medicine cabinet, and the cleaning materials we keep in the scullery. They took away a lot of things. Scouring powders, vermin killers, medicines. They said everything was being taken to be studied. I thought it must all have been brought here. I thought Mr Holmes was examining them.' She looked at me hopefully, but I was unable to say anything that might help her. 'They also wanted to know if anyone else lodging or living at the tavern, or any of our customers, had been taken ill recently. Fits and seizures, stomach aches. But no-one has, as far as we know.'

'Did they say what had prompted this action?'

'No. I was hoping you could tell me. Has our property come here for examination?'

I tried to adopt a soothing tone. 'I don't know, but it does seem very likely.'

'Has Mr Holmes told you anything?'

'No, I am afraid not. He is assisting Professor Russell, who is our senior professor of chemistry, and he has forbidden Holmes to reveal anything of their work until his report is made public.'

She uttered a groan. 'I think I can guess what the report will say, and why the police have descended upon us like this,' she said. 'Poor Summers, his death cannot have been a natural one, and they think he was killed by something in our house. But what it was, and how he came by it, we may never know. People will think we don't run a clean kitchen and poisons have somehow found their way into our food and killed that poor young man. We will have no custom, no lodgers. We could be ruined.'

I had no words of comfort to give her. She was a sensible lady who wanted information, not empty reassurances or platitudes. Fortunately, at this moment Holmes arrived, and she almost sobbed with relief to see him.

'Oh, Mr Holmes, thank goodness you are here,' she exclaimed. 'I do hope you can help us!' She briefly described to him the unexpected arrival of the police at the tavern, and the searches they had made of the premises.

He listened calmly, his features betraying nothing. 'I will do my best to help you,' he said. 'I regret that I cannot tell you what work I have been engaged in, but it would greatly assist me if you could describe anything the police have shown a particular interest in, and what questions they have asked you and your lodgers and staff.'

'Of course, I will help you in any way I can,' she replied. 'They wanted to know what materials we employ for cleaning the tavern and destroying vermin, and anything for medicinal use. They asked us where we buy them, where they are kept, and who might have used them. There is a cabinet in the gymnasium with the usual things for treating little cuts and so on. And there were liniments for the muscles. But there was nothing that might do anyone any harm. The cabinet is not locked. We don't provide anything for the boxers to take other than water, and a little brandy might be brought from the bar if needed. We don't give them medicines or tonics.'

'Who can go to the cabinet?'

'Anyone might. Calum won't allow any of the female staff into the gymnasium during classes as the men would find it too distracting, but they come in afterwards to clean.'

'Dr Wrothby's syrup was popular with the men, was it not?' asked Holmes.

'Oh, yes. Some of the men use it, but they buy their own, although it tastes very nasty. But then many people think the nastier the medicine, the more good it does, don't they? If the police have sent anything like that here, it could only have come from the lodgings.'

Holmes nodded. I noticed he didn't ask her precisely what items had been taken away, and I guessed that they were in the laboratory at Barts, under examination.

'Did the inspector ask you for a list of what you have used in the past? Either medicinal or cleaning materials? I mean any items that were not there today, but you might have had before?'

'No, he didn't.'

111

He gave her an encouraging look. 'You strike me as a lady with a keen eye for detail. I am sure that you could make such a list.'

She nodded emphatically. 'You are quite right, Mr Holmes. I keep a note of all our business stock, and still have the receipts for our purchases.'

'You mentioned vermin killers.'

'Yes, we keep a few packets. I get them from the chemist, Mr Fuller's. His shop is only a few doors from us. I always sign the poison book. Most businesses and homes have something of the sort. I mix the powder with a little butter or dripping and put it on some bread. I never leave the pieces anywhere where someone could take them by accident, of course. Under the floorboards, all the little places where vermin might go to run to their nests.'

'Where are the powders kept?'

'There is a drawer in the scullery.' She paused. 'I remember something else, now. The inspector wanted to know who could go into the kitchen. Of course, anyone living at the tavern or lodging with us could. The men who stayed here, they often went down to the kitchen for a cup of tea or cocoa. I'm not sure they ever went into the scullery, although they might have done. But it was obvious what the powders were — they were properly labelled as poison. No-one would take one by mistake.'

None of us mentioned the other horrible explanation of the young boxer's death, which must have been in all our minds — that Summers, in mortal fear, had made away with himself.

Mrs Shem fell silent, despondent at the invasion of her home and dreading the consequences.

'Let me know if there is anything else you can recall,' said Holmes, 'but I will go and see Professor Russell now and advise him of what you have said. His report will go before the inquest when it resumes.'

Mrs Shem was obliged to accept that this was all she would learn. She thanked us for our sympathy and promise of help, and returned to her beleaguered home, perhaps a little less unhappy than she had been when she arrived. Holmes made his way back to the laboratory, and I accompanied him to see what I might learn. But it was now very clear to me that the inquest would be told that Bill Summers had died from poisoning with strychnine.

CHAPTER TWENTY

'It was strychnine, was it not?' I said as we walked. 'I gathered that from the appearance of the body and the kind of materials the police were interested in.'

Holmes reluctantly grunted agreement, obliged to accept that concealment was no longer possible. 'You are correct, but you must say nothing to anyone else while our work is in hand. The examination of the body has established that the heart and other organs are sound and show no evidence of disease. Tetanus, which was a possibility, has been entirely ruled out. There is no injury on the body which might account for it. The stomach contents, however, reveal that Summers consumed a fatal dose of strychnine.'

'And what do the police suspect — murder, or suicide?'

'Either are possible. There have been cases of people taking vermin powders to destroy themselves. It is an act of desperation, and they can have no idea of the protracted agonies of such a death. I agree with Mrs Shem, that one would never take such powders by mistake. They are clearly marked as being poisonous, and most manufacturers colour them with Prussian Blue, or soot, so they do not appear at all appetising. From her description of where she placed the pieces of poisoned bread, I am confident that she very wisely located them where no person would have seen them, or if they did, they could not have imagined them to be something they might wish to consume.' He paused, and I wondered if he was determining how much more he could tell me. I understood the prohibition on making any revelations. With the cause of death now shown to be poison, and the prospect of a crime having been committed, the police did not wish to alert a potential suspect before the tavern had undergone a more thorough search.

Holmes made his decision, and I was grateful and perhaps a little flattered that he acknowledged I was to be trusted. In fact, from that moment on, I do believe that he kept fewer secrets from me, except of course those he retained out of a sense of mischief.

'The powders we are examining are particular to Fuller's chemists. He mixes his own and has a light touch with the colour. To make vermin powders, the pure alkaloid is used, combined with a large volume of flour and sugar. We received three packets, all of which were sealed.'

I saw why Holmes was anxious to have a list of stock from Mrs Shem. This might reveal that packets were missing, and Holmes had only been sent what remained.

'If such a thing was put in food or beer, it would be noticeable, surely?' I said.

'It would. The taste of strychnine is intensely bitter. I can attest to that, having sampled a single drop of its most dilute form, tincture of the nux vomica bean. A person given strychnine would undoubtedly detect that something was amiss. But it is possible to ingest a fatal amount before being alerted to the danger by the taste.'

'I take it there was nothing suspicious in the medicines?'

'No, we received one bottle of Wrothby's tonic, the property of one of the lodgers, which was the normal formulation. I also subjected the bottle of Dr Goode's tonic, the one I purchased, to a test, and while it is stronger than Dr Wrothby's it is not harmful in normal use. None of the other medical or scouring material submitted for analysis contained strychnine.'

When we arrived in the laboratory, we found Inspector Sturridge in conversation with Professor Russell, who was demonstrating the results of his work. I would rather not have encountered the inspector again, but it did seem inevitable. From his expression when he saw us, the sentiment was mutual and made all the worse for him by the fact that he had no authority to dismiss us from the room.

'Ah, you two again,' he growled. 'Well, you need not concern yourselves with this case any longer, because I have solved the mystery.'

'Kindly enlighten us,' said Holmes.

'Oh, I'm not sure if I should,' taunted Sturridge. 'I know you amateurs; you might try and take the credit for yourself.'

'I promise faithfully,' said Holmes, with great solemnity, 'and Professor Russell may like to witness this, that I will make no attempt to take any credit for your solution.'

'Please proceed,' said Professor Russell, who appeared similarly disinclined. 'You may speak openly before these gentlemen. I can vouch that nothing will be made public without your permission.'

'Very well,' said Sturridge. He addressed us, in the manner of an instructor delivering a lecture. 'It is clear to me that Bill Summers was murdered. You see Professor Russell has demonstrated without any doubt that Summers died from a fatal dose of strychnine. Now, you might ask how was a man murdered with such a thing? Well, the stomach also contained traces of iron sulphate and quinine, and these are known ingredients in a common tonic and stimulant used by sportsmen, which also contains a small quantity of strychnine. Was Summers induced to swallow a fatal amount of this tonic? Of course not. Why would he do such a thing? A strong young fellow like that, he would have had to drink a whole bottle or more to be in any danger. No. The killer must have laced a bottle of tonic with extra strychnine using a paper of rat poison, and then offered some to Summers. So, when Summers took what he thought was the usual dose, it contained enough strychnine to kill him. Of course, it had a bitter taste, but he was used to that. These tonics always taste bitter, what with the quinine as well. Now, I hear you say, why did he not notice the mixture was coloured blue from the rat powder? I will tell you. A very important clue, which you must have missed, is that there was no spoon in the room. That means he must have drunk it from the bottle and not noticed the colour at all. Many people do that. Even if it was extra bitter, he could have swallowed enough to kill him before he could stop.'

'Have you located the poisoned bottle?' asked Professor Russell. 'And the powders we were sent had not been opened.'

'No, well, I think the killer, having prepared the poisoned bottle, offered Summers a drink, friendly like, and then took the bottle away. He might even have pretended to drink some himself first to show that it was alright. There was plenty of time before it took effect on his victim for him to remove the bottle and destroy it. And the paper from the vermin powder would have gone on the fire. As to the culprit, well, there is no mystery about that. We already have him under our noses: Jim Jones, the man Summers was due to fight next month.'

'I see,' said Holmes, 'that is an elegant solution. Do you know what motive Jones might have had to murder Summers? He had the chance of earning a good purse at their match next month, which he has now lost.'

'I don't need to prove motive, Mr Holmes. But I am sure Jones will tell us when he confesses.'

'Have you determined why Summers took hold of the carving owned by Jones?'

'Ah, well, we cannot go into the mind of a dead man, but here is my theory. Summers, once afflicted with the pain of strychnine poisoning, might have imagined that Jones had cast an evil spell on him, his power coming from the ebony idol in his possession. Perhaps he thought the idol had worked its magic on the tonic mixture so it wouldn't harm Jones but would harm his enemies. So, he thought he could undo the spell by taking the idol and casting it into the fire. He goes to Jones's room to do so, and takes the idol from the chest, but before he can destroy it, he is seized with a fatal convulsion and expires. There. Now, if you will excuse me, gentlemen, I will return to the station to make my report, which I will place before the coroner. I intend to ask the inquest for a verdict of murder, naming Jones as the killer.'

And with a look of supreme satisfaction, Inspector Sturridge left the room.

CHAPTER TWENTY-ONE

Holmes and Professor Russell exchanged meaningful glances. Neither chose to express an opinion on Inspector Sturridge's theories or his intentions.

'We still have much work to do,' was all Russell would say, and Holmes set to it with alacrity.

I felt that my presence was not required and left them to their labours.

I decided that it would be useful to spend some time in the college library to enhance my scant knowledge of organic poisons. A recently published volume on forensic medicine offered some valuable information.

The *strychnos nux vomica* tree, which is found only in hot climates, produces poisonous seeds whose most powerful ingredient is strychnine. A liquid extract is derived from the seeds, and this is used to make the more dilute tincture. It would not do to confuse the two, since the concentration of strychnine in the extract is six times that of the tincture. The bitter tincture is an ingredient of a number of common medicines and would certainly have been used in the manufacture of both Dr Wrothby's and Dr Goode's syrups.

Strychnine, I realised, is one of those rare materials which on the one hand is a deadly poison, extensively used as a destroyer of vermin, and on the other, a highly regarded medicine suitable in small doses for human consumption. I already knew that it is considered to be a valuable tonic, stimulating the heart and respiration and enhancing athletic performance, although the precise nature of this function was imperfectly understood. Nowadays, tonic mixtures are produced in quantity by large companies and the strychnine content is carefully controlled, but in the 1870s chemists often formulated and manufactured their own mixtures with variable results, and a simple error in the dispensary could and sometimes did result in an accidental overdose. Strychnine has also featured as an agent in sensational murders. Even twenty years after the event, people still talked of the notorious Palmer case of 1856.

That evening, Holmes and I repaired to a nearby tavern with a quiet corner where a simple supper could be had, suitable for the purses of medical students, and Holmes was permitted to smoke a pipe.

'I cannot imagine why Jones would have wanted to cause any harm to Summers,' I said. 'I do not take him for a coward, and he had no reason to prevent the match taking place next month, which could have led to considerable advancement.'

'I agree,' said Holmes, pulling a paper bag of dark tobacco from his pocket. 'In fact, the only reason Jones is suspected at all is because Summers went to his room and tried to acquire the ebony idol. The current assumption is that he wished to destroy it in order to end the power he imagined it had over him. Whether that was no more than his fancy, or he had a real reason to think that Jones meant him harm, we cannot know. But Inspector Sturridge believes, without any proof, that Summers came to that conclusion because he might have accepted a dose of tonic mixture from Jones.'

'Baxter said that Summers disliked tonics and didn't take them.'

'Yes, although if he was particularly concerned about a forthcoming match, he might have made an exception.'

'What about — but no, that can't be it.'

Holmes looked at me quizzically.

'I had wondered if someone had placed a wager on the fight and simply intended to weaken Summers, but if they had wanted to do that, it would have been nearer to the date. In any case, it was not a fight that would have attracted larger bets.'

'I agree,' said Holmes.

'Have you discovered the origins of the poison?' I asked.

'Not yet, but we are eager to do so. Once we know that, it will assist us considerably. It is possible, as the inspector suggests, that an apparently innocent tonic was adulterated with vermin powder. Strychnine is not easily soluble in water, but it might well have been suspended in a thick syrup. The composition of the most commonly sold vermin killers, Battle's, is well known; they are twenty-three per cent strychnine mixed with flour, sugar and Prussian Blue. We have now established that Mr Fuller, the chemist of Covent Garden, uses a formulation something very near to Battle's, although he adds less dye. His powders each weigh five grains, of which one and a quarter grains are pure strychnine. Half a grain of strychnine has been shown to be fatal to an adult, and we estimate that Summers must have consumed about a grain. Recall also that Mr Baxter said that Summers had lost his appetite, and the post-mortem has confirmed that he had eaten only sparingly. He would have been more vulnerable to poison than usual. Wrothby's tonic contains only one sixty-fourth of a grain in a one-drachm dose. Goode's is twice that. The maximum dose recommended by physicians is one sixteenth of a grain.'

Holmes was using what we call apothecaries' measure, which is mainly employed by chemists and pharmacists. Even then it was not used or understood by the general public, and still less so today. One grain is, as one might imagine, a very small amount. A drachm, which is equivalent to a common teaspoon, is an eighth of an ounce, and there are sixty grains to a drachm. This means that twelve powdered vermin killers would have filled a single teaspoon and contained fifteen grains of the deadly strychnine.

'He would have had to add several of the powders to a bottle of tonic to result in a fatal amount from the usual dose,' I said.

'Indeed. The stomach contents have provided us with few clues, as flour and sugar are common enough and we are still looking for traces of dye. We are only grateful that the material was made available so soon after death, or we might have had a harder time of it.' Holmes had stuffed the unpleasant-looking coarse tobacco into his pipe, a rather handsome new briar I noticed, and proceeded to secure a suitable conflagration. 'I have had a long conversation with Professor Russell, who has many years' experience of the examination of materials in poisoning cases,' he went on. 'His knowledge of the strategies employed by poisoners is both extensive and illuminating. There is another possibility which he has offered for consideration. Many medicines are provided in the form of powders. If they are bitter, they can be enclosed in a wafer so they can be swallowed without tasting them. He suggested that Summers could have been offered such a thing and induced to take it. The murderer might even have swallowed a wafer himself, one he had secretly prepared containing only flour or sugar, and then offered the poisoned one to Summers. These wafers are composed of flour and water, intended to dissolve quickly and release their contents, so no trace would be found. One powder would explain both the death and our findings. The empty packet would be thrown on the fire, and then we wouldn't need to account for a missing bottle. Or indeed —' and here he gave a little smile — 'the absence of a spoon.'

'The difficulty is that we really can't say when Summers took the poison,' I said. 'I have been reading about it, and it seems that the initial symptoms might start only a few minutes after ingestion, or they could be delayed by as much as an hour.'

'And death within two hours of that,' said Holmes. 'Summers must have screamed in agony and called out for help, but the noise both from the tavern downstairs and the gymnasium above could well have drowned his cries.'

'We still have to consider a motive,' I said.

'But what if there was no motive?' said Holmes, thoughtfully. 'What if Summers was not the intended victim?'

CHAPTER TWENTY-TWO

I was somewhat taken aback by Holmes's suggestion. 'I'm not sure I understand,' I said. 'Do you mean the murderer intended to poison another person and poisoned Summers by mistake?'

'That is one theory, but here is another which Professor Russell has advanced, and it may have some merit. Suppose that this attack, if one can call it such, was not directed at an individual at all, but at the King Henry Tavern. More than that, it could even have been an attack on the sport of boxing. Mrs Shem feared that they could be ruined if it was thought that their food or drink had caused a death. There are, as we have seen, opponents to pugilism in all its forms who see the tavern, and others like it, as places that nurture and encourage boxing.'

'Surely they would not deliberately kill or injure others to advance their ideas?' I said.

'It would seem illogical, but then fanaticism knows no logic. The recent death of Bowman, after sparring with Jones who was lodging at the King Henry, has drawn attention to the place and made it a target.'

'But Bowman's death was not caused by boxing,' I protested.

'The opponents of boxing may choose not to believe that,' said Holmes. 'There is a medicine chest in the gymnasium to which the boxers had access when they needed it. Mrs Shem has said it did not contain anything meant to be consumed, but something might have been placed there, a bottle or wafers, without anyone's knowledge, with the intention of causing harm, and it just happened to be Summers who took advantage of it. If he disliked the taste of liquid tonics, he might well have been willing to swallow a wafer.'

'You are saying that someone was so determined to see the tavern closed down, that they didn't care how much harm they did or even who they harmed to achieve it,' I said, horrified.

'I regret that it is not impossible,' said Holmes. 'I have studied some of the more unusual crimes, and Professor Russell has had ample reason to do so. People have been known to place poison in foodstuffs when they wished to exact revenge for some slight. The motive might appear to our eyes to be quite trivial; often the criminal is a servant who has been scolded by her mistress. Such desperate persons have been known to poison entire households. They usually employ arsenic, since it is easy to come by, without a noticeable taste, and the symptoms can be blamed on consumption of spoiled food, or natural illness such as cholera. They might imagine it will do no more than cause discomfort, and they will have the pleasure of watching their victims endure stomach aches and other distressing symptoms. Sometimes, however, through their ignorance of the fatal dose, they kill.'

I gave this dreadful idea some thought as Holmes puffed quietly on his pipe. 'Who might have had the opportunity to put a poisoned bottle or wafers in the medicine chest?' I said. I realised, to my alarm, that there was a long list of suspects. 'Anyone employed at the tavern might have done so, or one of the men who exercise at the gymnasium or the members of a boxing club who meet there. How might we find this person? Inspector Sturridge thinks he already has his man, so he will not be making any enquiries in that direction. And if we suggest the idea, he will take no notice.'

'Undoubtedly,' said Holmes. 'I must pursue the question. Such people often give themselves away by their behaviour. Close and careful observation is required, and questioning which takes the form of general conversation will reveal much when the suspect's guard is down.'

'I am sure Professor Logan would be happy to allow you to question his employees, but the police would object if they found out, and Robson certainly would.'

Holmes smiled. 'Which is why I shall adopt a different method.'

I was more than a little apprehensive at this announcement. Past experience told me this could involve setting fire to things. 'What do you intend to do?' I asked cautiously.

'There are no further classes at Barts during the winter vacation, so I will be free to seek another occupation. Once the King Henry has re-opened for custom, I shall apply for the position of junior bartender. I am sure Professor Logan will be happy to oblige me, and of course his brother and Mrs Shem will be informed of my secret identity.'

'What about Robson?'

'Robson is chiefly concerned with the gymnasium. When he drinks downstairs, he favours the lounge bar. He has his armchair, which is so well used by him that the padding complies to his form. And he avoids the public bar, since he is afraid of encountering the ghost of Dr Wrothby. I will confine my work to the public bar and in any case, I will be disguised. If you address me when you are there, I will be Mr Sherrinford.'

I felt some concern at the prospects of success of this plan. If Robson did happen to notice the new barman and saw through Holmes's pretence, he might have organised a gang of seasoned pugilists from his circle of friends to make his objections clear.

Readers of Dr Watson's memoirs will know that in later years Holmes developed the skill of disguise to a fine art, such that even a good friend would fail to recognise him face to face, but the efforts that I had witnessed thus far were of a rather amateurish standard. Cheap wigs and false beards might have been suitable for a stage performance in a church hall but were not convincing under any closer inspection.

'Professor Logan mentioned that one of the barmaids was rather sweet on Summers. They might know something.'

'I have no doubt of it,' said Holmes. 'You recall Mrs Shem saying that females are allowed into the gymnasium when classes are over. They are not therefore exempt from suspicion.'

'If anyone in the tavern is secretly opposed to boxing, it is much more likely to be a woman,' I said.

'Yes,' said Holmes, grimly. 'I fear that Mr Sherrinford, in order to extract the information he requires, might be obliged to employ the wiles of courtship.'

I was somewhat aghast at this. I had already observed that ladies found him rather interesting, even when he gave them no encouragement whatsoever. 'Holmes, you can't mean it!'

'Oh, have no fear. I shall be discreet, no more than friendly, and then disappear.'

'Leaving broken hearts in your wake.'

He shrugged. 'I am sure they have battalions of admirers to take my place.'

I hoped he was right. We agreed to meet in the same location in two days' time to discuss progress. I awaited his report with trepidation.

CHAPTER TWENTY-THREE

The following afternoon, I was due for another sparring lesson and was pleased to find the King Henry open again. Since I arrived at the gymnasium from the coach yard entrance and did not pass through the bar, I was not able to observe Mr Sherrinford. I was sorely tempted to take a look but decided not to make any change from my usual route, as it might have drawn attention to the imposture.

When I arrived in the gymnasium, I wasn't too pleased to see Robson prowling about, although I thought he was unlikely to actually assault me in front of witnesses. He did, however, direct probing looks at me, and I could feel them like little hard-knuckled jabs, even when my back was turned. I was warming my muscles by working with a punch bag when he approached me. His expression was somewhat derisive of my efforts, and I could see he was not there to assist me or suggest any improvement.

'I hope you gave your nosey friend my message,' he said.

I paused. I wasn't sure what reply to make but decided that the fewer words I used, the less trouble I might attract. 'I did,' was all I said.

'He needs to know where he isn't wanted,' said Robson. 'Maybe he'll stay away from here from now on.'

I did think of pointing out that Holmes was receiving special lessons from Professor Logan but realised that that might lead to conflict. It also crossed my mind to tell him that Holmes was currently away visiting family for the festive season, but I didn't think the lie would fall convincingly from my lips and might only alert Robson's suspicions.

'Maybe,' I said.

He scowled and walked away. Fortunately, he had said all he intended to say and did not address me again. I took very great care to look about me on my way home, and arrived safe and unmolested, wondering how much longer the horrid situation would continue.

The next evening, Holmes and I met as we had appointed for an exchange of information.

He was in clean workaday clothes, smelt of beer and tobacco, and sported a chestnut wig and matching whiskers. Holmes, it has to be said, always had the aroma of tobacco about him, as so many gentlemen do, but that was usually intermixed with the scent of his customary shaving soap and hair cream, which were both absent that day. In keeping with his costume, he was smoking a clay pipe which was packed with a particularly strong mixture. His disguise was rather better than I had feared, and I could see that he had been to some trouble and expense to look more convincing than in the past. Naturally, I had no difficulty in recognising him, although I made some humorous pretence of not knowing him at first, which I do not think deceived him. Who would have thought that the humble man at the table before me, wreathed in noxious tobacco smoke, and making short work of a plate of bread and meat and a glass of ale, would one day be the most celebrated detective of all time?

I was relieved to discover that he was as yet not engaged to be married and did not anticipate that such an extremity would be required.

'But I have made a new friend,' he announced. 'The little servant Sally who makes up the fires in the morning and does the rough work. She has been an ornament to the tavern for more than three years. When I pleaded ignorance of the arrangements, she pitied the poor newcomer, took me under her wing and showed me around the premises. I now know that the matches are stored on a shelf in the scullery in a tin box. The vermin powders are, or were before the police removed them, in a box marked "rat poison", which is in a drawer in the scullery with some of the coarser cleaning materials. They are not kept in the vicinity of any foodstuffs, but anyone might have access to the drawer, which is not kept locked.

'Sally has strong opinions on the other residents of the tavern and is happy to share them. She revealed that Professor Logan is very popular, especially with ladies, and Mr and Mrs Shem are a most devoted couple, but she warned me against Mr Robson, who is often drunk and in a bad temper. I promised I would stay out of his way.'

'I wish I could stay out of his way,' I said. 'He hasn't threatened me again, but he told me he didn't want you at the tavern. I don't like his manner.'

'Robson's worst excesses of drink and melancholy are said to be a consequence of the death of his wife some years ago. Sally wasn't at the tavern then, but she is an avid collector of gossip from those who were. She revealed that the Robsons were a contented and affectionate pair, hoping to raise a family, but Mrs Robson injured her spine with heavy lifting, as a direct consequence of tavern work. For that Robson cannot help but feel some measure of guilt. An operation was performed, an unwise experiment by a pioneer surgeon to ease the muscles of her back, but it only made matters worse. She had to wear a steel brace and was often confined to bed in great pain for long periods of time.

'Dr Wrothby, for all his faults, tended to her without charge, doing what he could to make her comfortable and ease her pain, which was another reason why his noisy excesses were met with amused toleration. Over the years, her constitution declined and after much suffering finally failed altogether. Once again, Wrothby was on hand to do what he could to support the grieving widower. Robson feels the loss very acutely. Sally thinks that the ghost of Wrothby is a phantom of his endless suffering. He is only some semblance of his old self when advising and training promising young boxers.'

'I don't think he regards me in that light,' I said.

'Your persistence does you credit,' said Holmes. 'Ideally the brain and the body should act together as one. Neither should be neglected.'

It was a noble sentiment. In years to come, the demands of detective work would take their toll on even Holmes's iron constitution. Watson would come to chronicle exhaustion, a habit of employing stimulants, and even a total breakdown requiring absolute rest. None of these were a feature of Holmes's time at Barts, several years before his great fame. When I introduced the two men some while later, I believe that Holmes, with all his eccentricities, was one of the finest and most complete human beings I have ever known.

'More interestingly,' said Holmes, 'I discovered that little Sally used to be in service with Dr Wrothby, doing the rough work. It was she who gave evidence at Wrothby's inquest, and she had a great deal to say about that, including some important facts which she never told the court.'

And with that, Holmes charged his pipe once again.

CHAPTER TWENTY-FOUR

'I was not surprised to learn that Mrs Wrothby, despite her public show of grief, was privately relieved at the loss of her husband,' Holmes continued. 'She had once revealed that she was glad she was never blessed with children, or they would have had a hard life. There are scars on her person, the marks of ill-use, which she dares not show to anyone, but which Sally had seen by chance.

'Soon after Dr Wrothby died, the practice was sold, and Mrs Wrothby went away. Sally thought her mistress was hoping to move up in the world and employ a maid, a post for which she was not to be considered. But Mrs Wrothby was kind enough to find her work at the King Henry. Sally was already familiar with the tavern because she sometimes used to get sent on errands there taking liniments and dressings for the boxers. She also revealed that Mrs Wrothby liked to go there herself when she could, to make these deliveries. Sally's visits did not take her long, she simply handed the parcel to one of the barmaids and returned home, but when Mrs Wrothby paid a visit, it was always while her husband was out on his rounds, and she was often absent for quite a while.'

Holmes paused at this moment, and the implication of his words hung in the air. It was an indelicate subject, and he did not choose to elaborate, especially as the import was mere speculation without proof.

'Did Sally reveal which of the barmaids was sweet on Bill Summers?' I asked.

'There are three young persons of that description, as well as a cook and a scullery maid who are mother and daughter and do not live on the premises. Sally lodges with them nearby. I am told that Summers, even on that short acquaintance, was generally liked by all, as he was quiet and very polite, but that one of the barmaids, Mary, bursts into tears when his name is mentioned and won't talk about him. I am sure she has something to say on the subject, but what it might be will require some ingenuity to extract. Of the other two, Rose has romantic ambitions in a more senior place, and Tilda is already walking out with a young plumber and has no interest in a barman. I did make enquiries about Annie, the barmaid who was the last person to see Dr Wrothby alive as he drove from the coachyard, but she has since married and gone away.' He puffed reflectively on his pipe. 'And then,' he said, 'there was the unexpected visit of Mrs Taylor.'

'Mrs Taylor?' I said. 'I have not heard of that lady. Is she one of Mrs Arroway's friends?'

'I cannot say. Sally informed me that a lady of that name recently called at the coach yard entrance of the King Henry asking to see Professor Logan on a matter of great importance. She was admitted, and he agreed to speak to her privately. She was there for about half an hour.' There was another long, tantalising pause, while the pipe again received my companion's attention. I felt that Holmes was doing it deliberately. Perhaps he was testing me.

I was beginning to be familiar with his methods and spent a few moments in reflection. The vital information, I guessed, was not what he had told me but what he had omitted. 'What day was this?' I asked.

'Ah, well, that is one of the fascinating things,' said Holmes. 'The visit was on the evening of the same day on which Summers was found dead. The police had gone by then, and the chattering crowds who had gathered outside had dispersed. The tavern remained closed out of respect, as was the gymnasium. The event had drawn newspapermen to their doors, but they had been told to go. All was quiet. One of the barmaids, Tilda, heard a knock at the door and was told if it was a newspaperman he should be sent away, but then she went to find the professor, who was busy restoring to order what had been left in disarray by the police. When she told him that a Mrs Taylor had called, he did not hesitate or ask for further information, he agreed to see her.'

'Do we have a description of her?'

'We do, although regrettably, it does not include her face. Sally saw them go to the office to talk. The lady was thanking Professor Logan for agreeing to their interview. Respectably dressed, veiled, spoke quietly. Manner somewhat agitated. They went in and the door was locked. When Sally asked Tilda who the caller was, she said it was a Mrs Taylor. That was all she knew.'

'A private matter, then,' I said. 'It may have had nothing at all to do with the death of Summers.' Holmes smiled and I saw that there was more to be learned.

'Sally listened at the door. Unfortunately, the key was still in the lock, so the strategy of looking through the keyhole was unavailable. She was also unable to hear what was being said, as they spoke very quietly. When she heard the key turn, she was able to move away quickly so as to appear to be passing by. Logan saw her and told her to go and mop the kitchen floor, as it had been muddied by police boots. She obeyed, so did not see the lady emerge from the room.'

'You attach some importance to this visit?' I said.

'I do. You see, it preyed upon Sally's mind, because although she was not acquainted with a Mrs Taylor, she felt sure, even on the small amount of conversation she had heard, that she knew the voice and she knew the lady. Sally was quite sure that the visitor was none other than Mrs Wrothby.'

'Is she certain of that?' I said. 'I mean, didn't Professor Logan say that he had not seen her for a very long time? And that was after Mrs Taylor's visit took place.'

'It was,' said Holmes. 'So, we are left with two possibilities. Either Sally is mistaken, or Professor Logan, for reasons as yet unknown, has lied to us.'

I was considering the implications when Holmes went on.

'Sally is a confiding girl, if one speaks to her with the right attention. Once she had warmed to her story, I asked her about the inquest on Dr Wrothby. Her evidence had been brief, and she did no more than agree with the testimony of her mistress, as one might expect. I felt sure there was more to emerge, and so it proved. Servants are often curious to know about changes in their usual orders, and we know that Miss Sally has an enquiring nature.

'On the night Dr Wrothby died, her mistress had sent her to bed early. Did she really have no curiosity about the reason? The answer was that she did. Sally told me that when she was in her attic room, she looked out of the skylight, and saw Dr Wrothby in the stable yard sitting in his chaise. She thought he might be waiting for someone. Then her mistress entered the yard, saw her husband, and went up to him. Sally couldn't tell if any words were exchanged. Mrs Wrothby put a blanket over the horse, gave it some feed and went away. And Dr Wrothby stayed where he was. Sally watched for a time, but nothing changed, and so she went to bed. She said she was pleased that the horse was fed and warm, because it worked hard and knew its business. It used to bring the doctor home safely, even when he was drunk. Next morning, when she helped Mrs Wrothby carry the doctor's body indoors, her mistress showed no signs of distress, and the horse blanket and feed bag had been put away.'

CHAPTER TWENTY-FIVE

I was mystified. 'What curious behaviour. If true, it means that Mrs Wrothby knew that her husband had come home that night, but did not rouse the servant to help bring him indoors?'

'Precisely.'

I pondered this mystery. 'If she had not, as she claimed, gone to her bed early, she might have seen him drive by from one of the windows that face the street,' I said. 'When he did not come indoors, she would have suspected that something was amiss. Perhaps she thought he was drunk and needed assistance, and went out to look. When she did, she must have realised that he was beyond help, and nothing could be done. If she was feeling unwell, I suppose I cannot blame her for going to her bed and attending to the body next morning, but she might not have liked to admit that that was what she did.'

Holmes said nothing but drew pensively on his pipe, and I continued to reflect on what we had learned.

'If Sally is right, and the mysterious Mrs Taylor is the former Mrs Wrothby, then the widow has remarried,' I went on. 'In view of the professor's somewhat colourful reputation with ladies, I imagine he has chosen not to mention the interview because of the way it might be interpreted, however innocent the reason might be.'

'That is one explanation,' said Holmes. I waited to be told another but waited in vain. 'I have, however, been provided with a useful piece of information concerning the lady which I mean to pursue. Some clues lie in plain sight, if one only knows where to look for them. Did anything else of interest strike you about Mrs Taylor's visit to the King Henry?'

'I don't think so,' I said. 'Only that if she really is the former Mrs Wrothby, that would explain how she knew the location and the correct door to go to and who to ask for. And if she has moved up in the world and wishes not to be known for her earlier connection, then that would also explain her care not to be recognised. If she knows her first husband's secrets, she will be afraid that the knowledge of her former name might place her in danger. You must tread very carefully, Holmes.'

'You make some interesting points,' said Holmes. 'But you have not fully observed.'

I knew better than to press him to tell me more. 'Will you ask Professor Logan about his visit from Mrs Taylor?'

'When the time is right,' said Holmes. 'When I am surer of my facts. When his guard is down, and he cannot parry my questions. In the meantime, I have much still to learn at the King Henry as well as other enquiries to make, and I mean to write a note to Sergeant Lestrade, who may unwittingly be in possession of the vital piece of information which will prove or disprove my conclusions.'

Holmes was absent for a few days, which enabled me to spend more of my time in the company of my friend George Luckhurst, who was still attending classes at the gymnasium and sparring very skilfully. Luckhurst was employed as an assistant keeper at the British Museum, where he studied Greek and Roman antiquities, and an annuity left to him by a great-aunt meant he enjoyed comforts beyond the modest means of a medical student. His apartments near the museum were a haven of elegance, with good food and good conversation. As we dined one evening, I could not help but complain about Holmes's habit of only mentioning half his thoughts to me. Luckhurst knew Holmes's odd ways better than most, as they had been at university together. He listened attentively and kept the wine flowing. 'Half?' he said. 'As much as that? He hardly told us anything, and what he did say was almost impossible to understand.'

'He has got himself involved in some very strange business, and I would gladly unburden myself and confide my concerns to you, except that I am expressly ordered not to divulge it to anyone,' I said.

'You intrigue me,' he said with a smile. 'I have gathered from your occasional absences and preoccupied manner that Holmes has dragged you into his love of mysteries more than once. That encounter with the footpad — was that a part of it?'

I looked at him helplessly, and he didn't press me to say more. 'I promise I will write my memoirs one day, and then you will know everything.'

He smiled and raised his glass. 'I look forward to it.'

Nowadays, one of my greatest amusements is to watch the expression of astonishment spread across Luckhurst's face as he reads the revelations in these memoirs.

When Holmes reappeared at Barts, he rather crossly demanded to know where I had been, as if he thought I should always be available to assist him. I was about to protest when he added, 'I am to have a meeting with the three Furies. As before, it is uncertain which of us is more eager to draw information from the other. But I would welcome your presence, since my eyes cannot be everywhere and as I speak, I need to observe how all the ladies react to what I say. More can be conveyed by a brief change of expression than words; indeed, the face always tells the truth when the lips may follow with a lie. Oh, and since my rooms cannot be tidied and never will be while I am in residence, yours will be the most suitable private location.'

It was useless to raise objections and, in any case, I was curious to know more. 'What have you discovered?' I asked.

'You recall our visit to Goode's chemists' shop? I offered the young chemist a number of possibilities as to where Mrs Wrothby might be to see which one produced a change in his manner, and it was only at the suggestion that she might have reverted to her maiden name that there was any reaction. His response was an unusual one, not so much recognition as amusement, and he was very eager to suggest that I was correct. He must know that discovering a woman's surname before her marriage is not an impossible task. At the same time, I felt sure that the lady had taken considerable pains to ensure that she was not found and may well have asked Dr Goode's sons not to divulge anything they knew. My conclusion was that the chemist and his wife were well aware of her maiden name and were perfectly happy for me to pursue that quest, as they were sure it would not help me.'

I smiled. 'I am sure they were mistaken.'

'They were. If you have ever perused the records in Somerset House, you will know that an entry of marriage reveals only one partner of that marriage and does not supply the name of the spouse. It does, however, show the district in which the wedding took place, the volume number of the register and the page on which it is entered. It did not take long to discover that Dr Wrothby, fortunately a rare surname, married in the parish of St Anne's, Soho, in 1861. I could have applied for a copy of the certificate, which would have necessitated both an expense and a wait, but it was not necessary. I searched for the marriage of a Miss Taylor, of whom there were a great many, and found that a Miss Abigail Taylor was married in the same quarter of 1861 in the same parish as Dr Wrothby, and this wedding is recorded on the same page as his. The coincidence was too great. The chemist must have known that the lady's maiden name was one of the more common surnames. This does not of course assist me in finding her, but it does confirm that Professor Logan's clandestine visitor was Mrs Wrothby, using her maiden name as an alias. Unfortunately, Wrothby's death is too recent for the probate records to be publicly available, or I would have had an easier time of it.'

'So, Sally was correct.'

'I had no doubt of it. She had daily received her orders from Mrs Wrothby. One does not forget a voice under such circumstances. I also took the opportunity to look for the death of Mr Lunn but found nothing. If he is dead, then it will be recent.'

'Did you hear from Sergeant Lestrade?'

'He is undertaking searches on my behalf. The sergeant is not very imaginative, but he is dogged and determined, and may well rise further in the force. It is the last piece in the puzzle I am assembling and when I have it, and it fits, then I will have the full picture and I will spring my trap.'

CHAPTER TWENTY-SIX

When Holmes studied at Barts, he rented a two-room apartment near the British Museum in Montague Street. They might have been perfectly good rooms if he had not cluttered them with his collections of books and papers which were in no sensible arrangement that I could discern, and all saturated with the smell of twice-smoked tobacco. This, and his habit of practising the violin at all hours, meant that our friendship would never have survived sharing accommodation, despite the attendant economies. It was only when his courses at Barts were coming to an end that he sought a larger apartment, where he could assemble his own private laboratory so he might continue his experiments. I thought Watson was remarkably patient with him.

By contrast, however, my rooms, in a far humbler location, above a bootmaker's shop in Farringdon, needed only a little tidying of papers and the application of a duster before they were ready to receive visitors. To encourage conversation, which was often a strenuous and thirsty business, there were to be plentiful supplies of tea, and the sustenance of a plate of Abernethy biscuits.

Once the ladies had arrived and were settled from their journey, and had looked about them to reassure themselves that my abode was not a den of iniquity, I arranged for refreshments to be brought.

Holmes was quickly to business. 'Before we begin, I would like Mrs Goode to tell me something of her history. How did you become acquainted with Mrs Arroway and Miss Mitchell and become interested in their work to outlaw boxing?'

Mrs Goode did not appear to be well prepared for this question. She seemed to experience some discomfort and hesitantly glanced at Mrs Arroway and Miss Mitchell before attempting a reply.

'I think,' said Mrs Arroway, gently, 'that Mrs Goode, being a thoughtful and kindly lady, does not wish to place me and my sister in a position of being embarrassed by the story of how we met. I have no difficulty about that. Mrs Goode's husband is the eminent Doctor Jedediah Goode, and he is a generous and charitable man. Mrs Goode is his valued helpmeet in that she spends her days working tirelessly for the sick and needy, visiting their families to see how they might be helped to live wholesome and healthy lives. It was on such a visit that we became acquainted.

'It took place about a year or so after Dr Wrothby died, in the summer, I think, and Matthew required almost constant care. I felt no shame in accepting charity. I did it for his sake and that of my darling children. I told Mrs Goode the sad story of how a strong and active young man had been brought to that pass. Times were very bleak indeed. We could scarcely afford the medicines he needed. Mrs Goode was able to help us, and she also engaged the assistance of the Christian Mission. Jenny and I and the children go to their tea meetings very regularly now, and their readings are of great comfort. We have made many new and delightful friends.' She seemed about to say more on this cheerful theme but gave a little smile and stopped herself. I replenished the teacups.

'What we want to know,' said Miss Mitchell pointedly, 'is what progress you have made in bringing to justice the brute who killed my brother-in-law.'

Holmes nodded. 'I commenced my enquiries from the account given by Mrs Shem Logan regarding the boxer Lunn, and since then I have made every endeavour to find out what has become of him, so far without success. But this publication —' and here he extracted a copy of Mrs Arroway's paper from his pocket — 'conceals an allusion to another name. From this, I understand that you believe that the boxer involved in the bout with Matthew Arroway might have been another man, Professor Logan, who now teaches at the King Henry Tavern. Please correct me if I am mistaken.'

No-one corrected him. Miss Mitchell bit into an Abernethy biscuit with unnecessary vigour, as if it had annoyed her in some way.

'Would you care to let me know how you came to believe that?'

Mrs Arroway said nothing but looked at her friend.

I could not tell if Mrs Goode was necessarily expecting his question, but she appeared to be untroubled by it. 'I can answer that,' she said. 'It came about by chance. We had always believed that the man was Lunn, but then — well, as you know, Dr Wrothby died some three years ago and my husband thought it would be convenient to purchase the practice for when his eldest son, Robert, qualified as a surgeon. The two practices are not so very far distant, and he thought it would be a useful opportunity to build up Robert's list by referring some of his patients there. Patients who might not have wanted to consult Dr Wrothby,' she added, meaningfully. 'The premises required extensive redecoration, and the records were dreadfully untidy. I said I would help Robert order the papers. That was when I found — I'm not sure what one could call it. Not a diary as such, it was almost a memoir. It related to boxing, and in it there were all kinds of revelations about the involvement of Dr Wrothby in some very dubious events. I read a little, but it was very unpleasant, and I put it aside and thought no more of it.

'Some while later, when I met Mrs Arroway and heard her story, it had a familiar ring to it. I wondered, was this perhaps one of the events which Dr Wrothby had mentioned? I said nothing at the time, but later I searched amongst my papers and found that book. Now I think about it, I wonder if Dr Wrothby had kept those notes with the intention of blackmailing certain persons, or perhaps he intended to publish a scandalous memoir — anonymously, of course. We shall never know. But when I looked at it, I saw that he had written about poor Mr Arroway. Yes, he mentioned Lunn, who had been most disgustingly inebriated, but he also said that another man was involved in the horrible spectacle. And this was a man who would like his participation kept a close secret. A man, he claimed, whose name is not Lunn but is very similar. This man, he wrote, does not box nowadays, but there is a tavern in London where he may be found. He did not name it, but said that boxers are very welcome there, and it is the one tavern where he never has to pay for a drink.'

'You say it was thought this man was simply involved, rather than being the actual opponent?' asked Holmes. 'Was the nature of this involvement described? Did he arrange the match? Promote the match? Place wagers?'

'I am sorry, I have told you all I know,' said Mrs Goode.

'And you have deduced on this slim evidence that the man is Professor Logan?'

'When Mrs Goode told me of this,' said Mrs Arroway, 'I remembered that Dr Wrothby had preferred the King Henry, and always liked to make merry there. Where else could it be?'

'But wasn't Professor Logan out of London on the day of the Lunn and Arroway match?' I asked.

'So he claims,' said Miss Mitchell, with a sneer. 'But where is the proof? He might have been there, and all his boxing friends have lied for him.'

'At any rate,' said Mrs Goode, 'we can make no allegations based on a diary which fails even to name a name. I do not know what part he took.'

'Betting, I expect,' said Mrs Arroway sadly. 'It is the ruin of many a family, and a grievous sin.'

'I know nothing about the betting world,' I said, 'but if the fight had been stopped, or even not gone forward, because Lunn was unfit to fight, would Arroway have been declared the winner? I don't know who was favourite to win, but it might well have been in the interest of the betting men for the fight to go on. Is it possible that Lunn was given stimulants to strengthen him, and that it was this that led to the dreadful injury?'

'I would like to see this diary,' said Holmes.

'It was a horrid, disgusting thing,' said Mrs Goode. 'I destroyed it.'

'That is a great shame,' Holmes replied. 'I beg you, cast your mind back to your reading of it, and if there is anything you can recall which might be of value, write it down, and we will speak of it again.'

'Oh, please do!' exclaimed Mrs Arroway.

'You might have had in your grasp a document that would bring the entire boxing world to shame,' said Miss Mitchell, accusingly.

'I will do what I can,' promised Mrs Goode.

'You see how it is,' said Holmes, once our visitors had departed. 'I deduce that the widow Arroway has befriended a respectable gentleman at these tea meetings — single,

Christian, temperate, and not, I suspect, given to boxing. I wish her well.'

'Do you think Professor Logan was involved in the Arroway fight in some capacity?' I asked. 'He is a well-known figure, and it must be possible to prove where he was on that day.'

'I intend to do so,' said Holmes. 'But even if he was, as claimed, not in London, a man such as the professor may still have had influence from afar. There is, however, another man we are forgetting. The quiet man, the man who takes no direct action, the onlooker. He is also a Logan, and I think very loyal to his brother. Shem Logan is, and must have been for a long time, his brother's second in the ring. He is adept at doing what is needed to support a weary pugilist. And in the old bare-knuckle days, who knows what underhand tricks might have been employed to liven up a flagging boxer? The professor might well have had a financial stake in the fight. At the time, he was busy making money to purchase the tenancy of the King Henry. He might have placed a large wager on Lunn to win. He knew the quality of the men. He told us that he thought Arroway was too confident without the necessary skill to support that attitude, and that Lunn was hard to beat. It is possible that Shem Logan, either on his own account or at his brother's bidding, might have done whatever he could to give Lunn the best chance of victory.'

'But all they did was give him coffee to sober him,' I said. Then I had a sudden thought. 'Coffee is a strong enough flavour to conceal a great many other things. I don't know what boxers would use to sober up a man. But whatever their tricks, the professor would know them, and so would Robson.'

'Racing men are known to give stimulants to horses to make them run faster,' said Holmes. 'The principle is the same.'

'But if that is so, then both Logans must bear some guilt for the outcome, even if neither struck a blow. What a pity Mrs Goode destroyed the diary. Think what crimes it must conceal.'

'It may conceal very many things,' said Holmes. 'I wonder if anyone knew about Dr Wrothby's diary during his lifetime? Did he keep it hidden from his wife? Mrs Shem said that Wrothby used to boast about the damaging secrets in his possession. He might have given the impression that they were locked only in his mind. A man who makes such boasts is inviting trouble; any number of people might have wanted to silence him.'

'But apparently he never told,' I said. 'And died before he could.'

'But now,' said Holmes, 'I have further investigations to make as Mr Sherrinford, and in due course I will meet in private with Mrs Goode. Her claim to have destroyed Dr Wrothby's diary is undoubtedly untrue, but I will not challenge her at this point. I have given her the opportunity to consult it, and then claim to have recalled some of its contents. Then we will see what can be learned.'

CHAPTER TWENTY-SEVEN

Although Holmes had experimented with disguise many times before, his purpose had been to enable him to briefly infiltrate a situation with his true identity unsuspected. I believe this was the first occasion on which he had ever attempted an extended masquerade as another person. Naturally this gave me cause for concern, and I was more than ever anxious for our regular meetings, which not only advanced my information but reassured me that he was well and whole.

I did have one other anxiety, which I realise was unflattering to Holmes, and which I am somewhat ashamed to admit. However, should my readers also have had a similar idea, it would be best to express it now. Gentlemen who adopt a stance of strict virtue in public have been known to delve privately into scenes of licence under a false name, as if they have become different men. Holmes was so tightly in control of himself, such a stranger to emotion, so careful to distance himself even from thoughts of impropriety that I had to wonder if the same strictures applied to Mr Sherrinford? Would that gentleman plunge into dangers which he could only escape by transforming himself back into Holmes?

And then I had a rather daring idea. If Holmes could act like a secret spy, could I do the same?

The occupation of private detective is, I was to discover, one of the dullest in existence. It demands many hours of waiting at street corners, often in the worst of weather, while trying to appear as if present for some innocent purpose or even escaping any notice at all, while all the time keeping alert for a sight of one's quarry. The combination of watching while appearing to be not watching is a skill that few can carry off adequately.

Not having any disguise, I decided to appear as ordinary as possible, thus fading into the general crowd of persons in winter attire. I had a dark overcoat, a tweed cap, and a new muffler, which was a recent gift from my mother and which Holmes had never seen me wear. Many men were using their mufflers to keep chins and cheeks warm, and I did the same. A newspaper shielded me from wind and weather and gave me something to do. I was thus prepared for a vigil at the King Henry. Not that I was about to wait during the hours when I knew Holmes would be at work inside the tavern at the bar counter or in the cellars. There would be times when he was free from work, if only for half an hour or so, and that was what I was hoping to observe. I took up a position not far from the double doors and opened my newspaper.

Customers came and went, and delivery wagons rumbled into the yard. I saw Shem Logan and Mr Sherrinford unloading provisions and bringing them indoors. They set about their task without exchanging words.

I was longing for the warmth of the bar, where a comforting fire was ablaze, its brightness flickering through the windows, and was almost about to abandon my foolish attempt, when I saw Holmes emerge from the main doors. I quickly faded into the darkness of the carriage entrance. He was alone, and as he passed by, I slipped out of the shadows and followed him. He stopped and paused for a time outside Fuller's chemists' shop, studying the window display. Something had obviously caught his attention and he nodded, but did not go in. I expected him to return to the tavern, and concealed myself accordingly, but instead, he walked on. Around the corner was a wider thoroughfare lined with shops selling everything from household goods, linens and stationery, to costumes for ladies and gentlemen. One of the shops sold only mourning wear, since it was the fashion of society to match the heavy permanent pall of gloom adopted by Her Majesty. It was this emporium which Holmes entered.

When my mother buys haberdashery, the outing is more in the nature of a social engagement. She likes to go with a friend with whom she can converse about the news of the day. Together they will spend a pleasant time examining the goods on display before deciding what to purchase. The entire process might take an hour or two to complete, especially if rounded off by tea. Holmes, by contrast, had the decided look and purposeful gait of a man who knew exactly what he wanted and would waste no time in obtaining it. I anticipated he would emerge in a few minutes, and he did, holding a small paper bag, white with a black border, which he thrust into his pocket. He glanced at his watch and abruptly turned back in the direction of the tavern. I only just managed to blend into the shadow of a shop doorway in time. He walked quickly, and as expected returned to the tavern, but he did not go in. Instead, he entered the coach yard and waited, looking at his watch once more.

After a few minutes the rear door opened, and Mary crept out. She was wearing a warm jacket over her gown, a thick shawl, and a plain bonnet. Holmes greeted her with a smile. A few words were exchanged and then he took the little black bordered bag from his pocket and presented her with it. She took it shyly and opened it, drawing out the contents, a length of black ribbon. She coiled and twisted the little gift into a bow and held it to her bonnet to show how it might be used as a trimming, then she burst into tears.

And here I must report that Mr Sherrinford was the master of gentle understanding. He took no liberties, no familiarities, there was no touch of a hand or a shoulder, but simply softly spoken words. At length she dried her tears, and he offered her his arm. She placed her fingertips lightly on his sleeve, and they walked. I faded into the shadows once more.

They turned south towards the river and took a refreshing turn about the Victoria Embankment Gardens, a recent and welcome addition to the pleasures of London. As they walked, they talked, or to be more precise, Mary talked, and Holmes silently nodded. I knew they would not be absent long, as duty would soon call them back to the tavern.

I don't know where Holmes learned how to persuade people to talk. He was of course a diligent observer of human behaviour, and I expect his busy mind was constantly acquiring what he needed to know and put into practice, and, I feel sure, experience of what not to do. He noted the interests and habits of individuals, and what weight they gave to the vagaries of the world, and he used this information to create either provocation or sympathy, whichever was appropriate, in his constant search for the truth. So much of his life was a performance, that I sometimes wondered who the real Sherlock Holmes was.

I think I learned something that day. It was the value of listening. The gift of ribbon, so humble, so appropriate, had caused the poor girl to open her heart and express what had been troubling her, and as the words poured from her lips, Holmes listened. I think that was my value to Holmes: he could speak his thoughts, some of them at least, and I listened to them. It helped him assemble his ideas in a way that solitary thoughts, which he also employed when he felt them to be necessary, could not do. And Luckhurst, in his turn, listened to me as I expressed my annoyance with Holmes, saying little, but understanding.

CHAPTER TWENTY-EIGHT

On the following day, I received a curt note from Holmes to say that Mrs Goode had completed her notes on her recollections of Dr Wrothby's diary, and her visit to discuss the result had been arranged for that evening. A brisk flick of the duster was all that was needed to render my rooms suitable for a lady.

Holmes arrived shortly before the appointed time. I wondered if he would reveal to me the result of his perambulation with Mary, but all he did was settle into an armchair and study his notebook, which enclosed a slip of paper with a scrawled message. I felt sure that I would learn what progress he had made in his enquiries before too long, but I did not ask him, for fear of revealing my adventure. The more I thought about it, the more convinced I became that he would not approve of my spying on him. After a while, he leaned his head back in a contemplative pose, and I saw his eyes move about the room. Then he frowned. I wondered what had caught his attention. As far as I was aware, nothing in my parlour had changed in any significant way since his last visit. I could not help but look around myself. I had not purchased any new books or altered the arrangement on my shelves. Everything was the same. My overcoat hung on a hook on the door where it always was, ready to hand before I went out. And then I saw it. The new muffler, the gift from my mother, was with my coat.

A feeling of dread flowed coldly through my veins. I knew beyond a doubt that Holmes had seen the man in the muffler following him, and he now knew what he might well have previously suspected, that I was the man. I waited for him to make an observation, but he did not. What he thought of my escapade he never revealed, but if it had annoyed him my punishment was to remain forever on tenterhooks as to his reaction.

Under the circumstances it was something of a relief when Mrs Goode arrived for her interview. Her demeanour was calm and formal, like the secretary of a business meeting who anticipated concluding matters smartly. I offered tea, but this was declined, presumably on the grounds that our work would be completed before the kettle had had time to boil.

She had brought with her a folded sheet of notepaper and a printed leaflet which we had not seen before.

'My friends have been at work with great objects in mind,' she said. 'I will show you our new publication, but it is not yours to keep, as it is only to be passed to ladies.'

Holmes and I perused the leaflet, which announced the formation of The Ladies' Anti-pugilism League, which was to be launched upon the world very shortly. It listed the dates and locations of several public meetings. Ladies were welcome, but men were strictly excluded. The principal officers were Mrs Arroway and Miss Mitchell. The main object of the League was to organise a petition to be brought before Parliament to outlaw boxing altogether. Holmes returned it to Mrs Goode without comment.

'I have, as you requested, given considerable thought to all I can recall of the infamous diary of the late Dr Wrothby,' said Mrs Goode, 'and I have made notes of the result.' She unfolded the sheet of notepaper, which bore a disappointingly brief paragraph. She did not hand it to us, but after studying her work, she launched into a kind of paraphrase. 'Wrothby stated that he was present at the dreadful spectacle of the fight between Mr Lunn and Matthew Arroway. This took place in rooms above a tavern, which was a common refuge of persons interested in boxing. He did not name the tavern, but we know from Mrs Shem that it was the Two Spires. Lunn arrived the worse for drink and he had injured himself after a fall in the street. The landlord, and I believe the comment here was "I will not record his name as he would not thank me for it," or some similar words, insisted that the bout should proceed, as a large gathering had already paid their money to see it, and would not take kindly to being cheated either of their money or the fight. Wrothby did his best to ensure that the man was able to fight, but it was a bad business. He also stated very clearly that another man played a prominent part in the affair. As a recompense, from that day on he never had to pay for drinks at a certain London tavern.' She folded the paper. 'It is my contention that Dr Wrothby was receiving the reward of his silence.'

Holmes considered this brief account. 'We know that Dr Wrothby favoured the King Henry Tavern, but his comments do not, as you and your friends have suggested, prove that Professor Logan was involved in the Lunn and Arroway fight,' he said. 'It may refer to the fact that his brother Shem, who we know was present, since he tended the bar at the Two Spires, assisted Dr Wrothby in making Lunn fit to fight. Moreover, his actions were carried out under the orders of his employer, Mr Meaney, and I doubt that he can be blamed for that.'

'I am sorry, but I have nothing more to tell you,' said Mrs Goode. She gathered her materials in preparation to depart.

'Oh, but you have a great deal more,' said Holmes, leaning forward intently, 'and I beg you to remain. Mrs Goode, before we go on, and we really must go on, I wish to reassure you that it is no part of my intentions to expose to the world secrets that a lady might wish to remain hidden. What we discuss here is only in the interests of finding out the truth.'

I had no idea to what Holmes was referring, but when I glanced at Mrs Goode, she was not merely startled, but alarmed.

She quickly composed herself. Escape was possible, and I do not think either of us would have tried to prevent her had she attempted it. It might have crossed her mind, but after a brief interlude, she made her decision and steeled herself to remain. I sensed that she needed very much to know what Holmes already knew. I wondered if I should order tea after all.

'I would not insult a lady. I speak only to the facts, and the plain facts are that you have lied to us more than once,' said Holmes. 'The statements you have made to us have from the very start been a tissue of concealment and misdirection. But you have made significant slips which alerted me. It only remained for me to obtain firm proof of what I originally suspected, and that I have now done. Please do not attempt empty denials of what you know to be the truth. To begin, I do not believe that you have destroyed Dr Wrothby's diary. You know its value; it is a highly damaging document that you might one day seek to use for your own advantage. But you are keeping it hidden, because it also contains comments which you would not want me or your new friends to see. It would reveal that you were once the wife of Dr Wrothby.'

I was speechless with amazement. Only Holmes's tone of utter certainty prevented me from exclaiming in protest. Then I saw that the colour had fallen from the face of our visitor. She turned away her head so we could not see her anguish. But she said nothing, denied nothing. She must have known that would be futile. That was when I knew it was true.

CHAPTER TWENTY-NINE

Holmes continued with neither sympathy nor remorse. 'I will explain what alerted me. When you told us that Dr Goode purchased Dr Wrothby's practice, you spoke of Robert Goode as "his eldest son" and not, as I would have expected a fond and proud mother to claim, "our eldest son". It was a small slip but highly significant. But I suspected you long before that. At our first meeting, you tried to extract from me details of the investigation of the death of Bill Summers. You knew, before the full account was printed in the newspapers, that a young boxer had died at the King Henry Tavern, but you dared not reveal how you knew. You also failed to ask me the name of the deceased or anything about how the body had been found. This was because you did not need to ask. You already knew. Your explanation, which included how you knew of my involvement, was that you had learned of it by chance when reporting Bowman's death to the police as a case of murder. However —' and here, Holmes opened his notebook and extracted the message from its pages — 'I have established beyond doubt that no such visit or report was ever made. There was only one lady who was not employed at the King Henry who would have known about the death of Bill Summers, and the fact that I had been asked to look into it, and that was the same woman who on the evening of the same day when the body was found, paid a visit to the King Henry under the name Mrs Taylor and spoke to Professor Logan. That woman was you. Of course, I needed to confirm my suspicions, and I was able to use public resources, such as Somerset House and parish records, to be certain of what I already knew. Your marriage to Dr Goode, a widower with two sons, is quite recent.'

Mrs Goode seemed to shrink, all her strength and dignity gone. Tears flowed freely down her face, and she made no attempt to conceal or dry them. 'Few people know what I suffered as the wife of Dr Wrothby,' she whispered. 'No-one will ever truly know all of it. Some men are kind, and some are cruel. People imagine that boxing men will be rough and rude, while a doctor is gentle and considerate, but that is not always true in either case. Dr Wrothby, as I discovered too late, was the worst man I have ever known.'

'How did you meet?' asked Holmes.

'My father was a chemist. I worked for him in the dispensary, and at the counter. I made extracts, mixtures, lotions, pills; I knew the business well. The work I did in fulfilling Dr Wrothby's requirements impressed him. Our union was not love, but business. He valued my skill. I accepted him because I thought marriage to a doctor was a step up in the world, but it was not, it was a journey to the depths. After he died, I became housekeeper to Dr Jedediah Goode. I lived quietly and put behind me all that had gone before. A year later we were married. I have a new name and a new life.'

'I hope,' I said, sympathetically, 'that you are more fortunate in this new life.'

She managed a slight smile. 'My husband is strict but fair. He believes it is below his dignity to have a wife who works, even in a dispensary, and certainly not at a shop counter. I busy myself with visits to the poor, and I belong to ladies' charity committees, raising funds by sales of work. We make donations to hospitals and orphanages.'

'But you could not entirely escape the name of Wrothby,' said Holmes. 'I can well understand that you did not want Mrs

Arroway to know of it. Had it been suggested that the tonic to which Dr Wrothby gave his name had played some part in the death of Bowman, there might have been an enquiry which would have led to you and might have exposed you.'

'You are correct, Mr Holmes. That was my fear.'

'You mixed the tonic for Dr Wrothby, did you not?'

'I did. And I was confident that the result of my work was pure and without fault. After Wrothby's death I sold the right to a Mr Fuller of Covent Garden, to continue its manufacture under the Wrothby name, as it remained very popular. How he makes it and labels it is up to him. It is the name that purchasers trust, and it still sells. But people do have old bottles on their shelves. Bottles which I had prepared and labelled. It was just possible that Bowman had one of those. I knew Bowman, and I knew he took the tonic before a fight. Even though I was sure he could not have been poisoned by such a small dose, I was afraid that people might think that and ask questions.'

'You did not take any of Mr Fuller's products to the King Henry?'

'No, why would I do so after my husband's death? In fact, Jedediah hoped that his son's tonics, sold under the name of Dr Goode, would find favour instead, and told me that if anyone was to ask, I was to recommend them.' As she spoke a cloud briefly crossed her features, but then she quickly recovered herself. 'But he said that it was not appropriate for me to visit that place, and I did not go there again until recently.'

'That was the day you went to the King Henry calling yourself Mrs Taylor, which you did to discover more about Bowman's death.'

'Of course I couldn't use my married name, neither would I ever call myself Wrothby again, but Calum —' she gulped — 'Professor Logan knew that my father was a chemist called Taylor. I hoped he would realise it was I and speak to me.'

Both Holmes and I decided to ignore that slip.

'You consulted Professor Logan, even though you suspected he might be involved in some way in the death of Matthew Arroway?' asked Holmes, pointedly.

She straightened in her chair, some of her customary strength and defiance returning. 'I did. I know him to be a good man. In the past he has done things that were not approved of, and those old prize ring fights were not legal, but he has never, as far as I know, stolen or cheated, or injured any man except in fair fight. The diary left so much open to interpretation, and I decided that it was time I knew the truth. I felt sure that he would tell me.'

'What did he say?'

'He said he had not been present at the fight between Lunn and Arroway. He had been away, and he had papers to prove it, which he showed me. That night he fought a match in Manchester for a good purse. It was advertised and later recorded in one of the sporting newspapers, and he had cut out the pieces and kept them. It was conducted in keeping with the Queensberry Rules and while the police kept a watchful eye for possible infringement, they saw no reason to interfere. So, the police could also bear witness that he was there. And he won,' she added, with a lilt of pride in her voice.

'I accept that he was not at the Lunn and Arroway fight,' said Holmes, 'but might he have had an interest in it? Did he arrange it, or wager on it?'

'Not to my knowledge. As far as I know, it was the landlord of the Two Spires who arranged everything that took place there. But I remember that night, because Wrothby was very late home. He came back demanding hot soup and bread and ale, and in an even fouler mood than usual. He said he had been present at a fight where there were serious consequences. Both men had been injured and he had had to attend to them. He thought one might die. Since the arrangements were most probably unlawful, there might be a prosecution. But the newspapers never got to hear of it. Everyone made sure of that. He didn't tell me the men's names but later, when I read his diary, I knew which fight it was by the date.'

'He didn't tell you more?'

'I knew better than to ask.'

'When you last spoke to Professor Logan, he must have told you about the death of Summers?'

'Yes. I had tried to see him earlier, but the police and the crowds were still about, so I knew something terrible had happened and that frightened me still more. Later, when it was quiet, I went back. He told me about Summers and the dreadful appearance of the corpse. I suggested it might be lockjaw, but I dared not mention my other suspicions.'

'Summers did not, as far as is known, take any tonics as he did not like the taste.'

Mrs Goode smiled. 'Yes, many people objected to that. In fact, that was a good thing in some ways, as it would be hard for anyone to take too large a dose by accident. Wrothby's tonic is quite bitter. Only a very determined person could drink a harmful amount. But then people have been known to swallow vermin powders. That does not mean we should not sell them.'

'Indeed,' said Holmes thoughtfully. 'I have one more question to ask. Was it one of Dr Wrothby's edicts that you wait up for his arrival home at night, however late he might be?'

'It was. He was often quite inebriated, and the servant and I had to help him to bed.'

'Which you dutifully did, every time he required it, apart from the one night on which he died.'

'What do you mean?' she demanded.

'I mean that at the inquest, you stated that you had gone to bed early before he arrived home and did not find your husband's body until the next morning. Given what you have told me of him, surely you must have known that it would arouse his displeasure if you were not there to do his bidding? I would imagine you would have looked out for his return as you usually did. You would have seen the chaise pass by in the street before it entered the stable yard.'

Mrs Goode bent her head but said nothing.

'What did happen that night?' Holmes persisted. 'You had sent the servant to bed before the usual time, and you were alone to do as you pleased. Perhaps when you did so, you had already discovered that your husband was home but had not come indoors. You thought he might be drunk and still sitting outside in the chaise. You suspected, even hoped, that a cold night spent in the open might put an end to your unhappiness. Having made sure that the servant was not about, you went out to examine your husband's condition. You would have tended to the horse, which, like yourself, was an innocent creature which deserved better treatment. And then you went to bed. Next morning, the cold and the alcohol had done their work and you pretended to discover the body.'

Mrs Goode had by now fully recovered her poise and dignity. If there were accusations to be made, she looked prepared to fight them. 'You forget, Mr Holmes,' she said, severely, 'that at the inquest, Jedediah testified that Wrothby was probably beyond help on his arrival home that night. He attached no blame to me.'

'Any blame was impossible to prove,' said Holmes. 'Gallantry demanded that the grieving widow should receive the benefit of any uncertainty.'

'And as you are a gallant gentleman, I trust that you will grant me that courtesy,' said Mrs Goode.

Holmes merely bent his head out of politeness. 'I would do no less,' he said. 'And I must reiterate, what you choose to tell your friends about your past, I leave entirely up to you. I will not disclose it without your permission.'

'Thank you,' she said.

'Please commend me to Mrs Arroway and her sister. I wish them a happier future. Am I correct in deducing from Mrs Arroway's noticeable happiness, that she has met a worthy gentleman at the Christian Mission who has earned her approval?'

'That is correct. He is quite devoted to her, and he is disabled so can never engage in boxing, which in her eyes makes him especially interesting.' Mrs Goode rose to her feet. 'And now I must leave you.'

There was no suggestion that she was still required to stay, and she departed, head held high.

Holmes watched her go, then shook his head in regret. 'The lady has secrets still,' he said, 'but I mean to have them.'

'Do you really think she simply allowed her husband to die?' I asked.

'One bruise to his temple was fresh,' said Holmes. 'And although Wrothby was drunk at the King Henry, he was in a maudlin rather than aggressive mood. No-one mentioned a fight or a fall. Unfortunately, the barmaid Annie, who saw him drive away, is no longer here to be questioned, since she has married and gone away. I have learned that she was friendly with Mary with whom she shared a room, but was so enamoured of her prospects she failed to mention where she was going.' He grunted in annoyance at the romantic susceptibilities of womankind which impeded his enquiries. 'We do not know when Wrothby received that blow, or how damaging it was, and most especially, was it the result of an accident, or if not, who delivered it?'

CHAPTER THIRTY

The next time I saw Holmes at Barts, he was in one of his more irritable moods. He had completed some experiments in the chemistry laboratory and the results were not to his liking. He paced up and down with frown lines cutting through his usually smooth, pale forehead, and I decided not to interrupt him as he bellowed his frustration.

'I thought I had the answer, Stamford! I told myself I had been a fool to miss the obvious answer! Mrs Goode has told us that Wrothby's tonic was only ever produced as a syrup, and unlike so many of her statements, I have no reason to believe that is untrue. We know that Summers did not like the syrups, and even if he had been persuaded to try a dose, he would not have consumed a large quantity. It would have been hard, even if the syrup had been contaminated, for him to receive a dangerous amount of strychnine. But then I recalled the tiny clue, the fragment of wood chip found in his room, and the fact that after Wrothby's death the syrup was made under that name by Fuller's, the chemist in Covent Garden, where the boxers and athletes liked to buy their strengthening mixtures. I wondered if Mr Fuller had produced his product in the form of pills, to which Summers would not have objected? I went to Fuller's and lo and behold, he did sell Dr Wrothby's preparation in the form of pills and sold them in little chip boxes. I had imagined at first that the fragment I had found was from a matchbox, but I now believed it was from a chemist's chip box, a piece of which must have fallen as it was crushed in the hand before being thrown on the fire. We and the police have been hunting for a bottle which never existed.'

Holmes paused in his pacing and threw himself onto a bench stool. His new conclusion certainly sounded promising, but I could see from his behaviour that it had not proved to be so.

'I paid a visit to Mr Fuller and purchased a box of pills, which contained twelve,' Holmes continued. 'He was happy to share his wisdom and discussed the recent events at the King Henry with a clear conscience. I asked him if he had ever seen Summers in his shop purchasing any tonic either in syrup or pill form, which contained strychnine, or even vermin killers. Fuller said he had never seen Summers in his shop, and no person of that name or description had ever signed the poison book. Mr Fuller told me that the boxers never purchased the pills, which they disdained as the preference of elderly ladies and invalids, but they did buy the nasty-tasting syrup, an altogether manlier product.

'I therefore took another line. I wondered if Summers had obtained the pills from another purchaser. The answer is, he did. Fuller told me that one of the barmaids at the King Henry had bought a box of pills quite recently. His description was sufficient to identify Mary, the very person who we were told wept bitterly whenever poor Summers's name was mentioned.

'I have been making considerable and wearisome efforts to gain Mary's confidence. Yesterday I escorted her to Summers's funeral, where I thought it most likely that the homilies of the service would induce her to reveal what was preying on her mind. It was hard work, Stamford; she trembled long on the brink of confession. I eventually had to say that I had been told that she had bought pills from Fuller's and wondered if she had given any to Summers. She was obliged to admit the truth. She said, however, that she had only ever purchased the one box, at his request, and had seen him take four pills at once without any ill-effect. I was able to reassure her that although this was twice the dose advised on the label, he would not have come to any harm.'

This suggested encouraging progress, but my hope was soon dashed by Holmes's vexed expression. He took a few moments to reflect on the contents of his notebook, before tossing it dismissively on the bench.

'Today I have completed my analysis. The answer is plain. Even if Summers had taken leave of his senses and swallowed all twelve pills together, the total strychnine ingested would not have been a fatal dose to a strong young man. I have also subjected both Fuller's chip box and the fragment I discovered in Summers's room to examination under the microscope. It is clear to me that they are of different manufacture. My theory must be abandoned until a better one appears.'

I coughed gently, and he looked up at me. 'What if someone bent on murder prepared a pill, a single pill with a fatal dose? Then it could have been introduced into the box used by Summers.'

'That is possible, but it assumes that Summers was the intended victim, which is still uncertain. But making a pill in the manner of a chemist, one that would be good enough to resemble the others in the same box, is a skill known to only a few persons.'

I had not learned to make pills myself, but I was aware of how it was done. The medicinal ingredients had to be bound together with a thick syrup to make a mass stiff enough to be worked like clay. The mass was then rolled by hand into a long, even rope and divided into equal parts using a grooved pill machine. Each portion was then carefully rolled into a sphere and left to dry. I had to agree with Holmes. Only a person trained in a dispensary would be able to create a convincing-looking pill which would exactly match the ones made by Fuller.

'Even if this were possible, it leaves us with other questions to which I do not yet have the answers. Who had access to the box of pills in Summers's possession, or even knew he had such a thing? He seems to have told no-one about it, certainly not the other boxers. Only Mary knew he had it. And we are still left wondering about a motive. Mrs Goode has a dispenser's skill, but she had neither access nor motive. Another explanation is that Mr Fuller or his assistant might have made an error when preparing the pills, such that taking one or two would have resulted in unpleasant symptoms and four would have constituted a fatal dose. But he would have made a larger number at one time than just twelve, enough to fill several boxes. He was adamant that there have never been any complaints about his product, but even if it did happen that way, we cannot prove it, and Jones remains under suspicion.'

I was obliged to agree. 'Might Summers have asked another person to get another box of pills for him? Or gone further afield to buy them himself?'

'We have no evidence of either. He certainly did not go out that day. The weather was wet, and his boots were not. The mud on the soles was dry and several days old. He is not very assiduous in cleaning his boots, and some of the mud did not originate in London. One thing I am almost sure of, however. While we do not know precisely when Summers took the fatal dose, I believe he took it while he was in his own room. He was not poisoned in Jones's room. In fact, it is probable that when Professor Logan last saw Summers and asked him to come and exercise, the fatal dose had already been taken, and he was feeling the initial effects of the poison. Logan said he found Summers looking very nervous and restless. That might have been the first indication. I think that the dose was taken at some time during the hour preceding that conversation.'

I gave this some thought. 'The professor said that Summers seemed fearful and unsettled. He knew that Summers had been worrying about the forthcoming bout ever since Bowman's death, so he simply put it down to a fit of anxiety. But you are right, Holmes; from what I have been reading, that could well have been the early symptoms of poisoning with strychnine.'

'Yes, it is only later that the convulsions and lockjaw set in. Summers would have been in great pain, suffering alone, with nobody able to hear his cries. The state of the bedclothes — recall that the professor suggested an indelicate reason for their condition. But it could well have been caused by Summers lying alone on the bed and convulsing in his agony. Everyone was either in the gymnasium or the downstairs bar. Who could help him?'

'There was a scratch on his head,' I said.

'Yes, which was not made by the deceased. There was nowhere in Jones's room he could have suffered that injury. He was lying with his head on the rug which was slightly smeared with fresh blood. But on the floor in Summers's room there was no rug, and I saw a nail protruding slightly from one of the floorboards. I think he left his bed to try and get help, and then collapsed again. The body when afflicted with strychnine convulsions will bend like a bow, sometimes resting only on the head and the heels, and I think his scalp was cut by that nail.'

'What I don't understand is how and why he came to be in Jones's room,' I said. 'Did he really imagine that the ebony idol had harmed him and wanted to destroy it? He was clutching it very strongly. Was that because of his seizure?'

'Yes, it was clasped to his chest,' mused Holmes. 'Inspector Sturridge has assumed that Summers intended to destroy the idol, but if he believed it to be harmful, would he have held it so close? Was that merely a symptom of a seizure or something more meaningful? If I was to suggest the latter, I am sure Sturridge would dismiss my idea and say that the posture was of no importance. We cannot ask a dead man, of course, but I have the feeling that lacking any help, any relief, any cure for his pain, he might have recalled that the idol was reputed to have healing powers, that it strengthened Jones and cured his ills. Did he imagine it might do the same for him? In the brief respite between convulsions, before exhaustion set in, before the final paralysis, he must have staggered or even crawled to Jones's room and sought the only thing he thought might help. He was struggling to breathe, and so pressed it to his chest in the hope of relief.'

CHAPTER THIRTY-ONE

I was pleased and not a little relieved when Holmes advised me that Mr Sherrinford had completed his enquiries and left the King Henry to find other employment. I did not expect to encounter that gentleman again, but as it so happened I did, although it was many years later and in an unexpected place. But then Holmes always delights in the unexpected.

It was the morning of the resumed inquest on Bill Summers. Inspector Sturridge, who must have already made his opinions known to the coroner, arrived accompanied by two constables, in anticipation of crowning the day with an arrest.

Jim Jones was there, flanked on either side by his father and Mr Stockdale. I could not overhear their conversation, but it was easy to gather from tone and gesture that they were trying to encourage him that his chances of walking from court a free man, were good. Harry Baxter, whose bluff manner might have concealed a fatherly feeling towards the deceased, was in attendance, and he also had a brief word, which was well received. Professor Logan and Mrs Shem were there, but none of the other employees of the King Henry were in attendance. Mrs Goode, heavily veiled, but identifiable to those who knew her, was also in place, and watching carefully, gathering more grist for the mill of the newly formed Ladies' Anti-pugilism League.

The first evidence to be placed before the court related to the last time Summers had been seen alive and the discovery of the body. Professor Logan and Jim Jones were both invited to have their say, and we learned nothing new. The police surgeon we had met, the man who had imagined Holmes and me to be stretcher orderlies, then described his initial examination of the corpse.

Mr Baxter, as the man who knew the deceased best, was questioned closely as to whether he thought the young boxer was afflicted with melancholy. Baxter described Summers's nervous and superstitious nature, his distress at the loss of his lucky sixpence and his fear of the ebony idol, but denied very strongly that he had ever spoken of destroying himself. 'A young boxer, healthy and sober, at the very start of his career, with all the support and advice he needs, is not about to do anything foolish to avoid a bout,' he said. 'I have no doubt at all that in time, we would have come to an arrangement to suit everyone.'

'This ebony idol is a very interesting item,' said the coroner, once Baxter had returned to his seat. 'Might we see it?'

An officer who had brought the carving to court in a linen bag came forward, drew it from its wrapping and set it on the evidence table. There was a distinct creaking of seats and rustle of garments as onlookers leaned forward, necks craned to get the best view.

The coroner spent some moments in contemplation of the exhibit. 'I confess I do not see anything in this which might excite alarm,' he said at last, mystified. 'Mr Jones senior, I understand you carved this — um — idol, as it is called? Could you please come forward and tell the court what it represents?'

Mr Jones senior obliged. 'I have been making traditional carvings of this nature for some years,' he said. 'This one was made as a gift for my son. It portrays a tribal elder of West Africa from where my ancestors were taken to be sold as slaves. To me, it personifies calm, wisdom, patience, firmness, strength through adversity, remembrance of the past, and faith in the future.'

'So, do I gather that its purpose is to inspire wholesome thoughts, and is not in itself a religious object?'

'That is correct.'

'Thank you, Mr Jones, you may step down.'

We next heard from Surgeon Stevens. He had conducted the initial post-mortem which had ruled out tetanus, injury and natural disease as causes of death. He listed the samples of bodily fluids and organs which had been sent to Professor Russell for analysis.

Professor Russell was next to give evidence, and the court fell silent. His statement was the whole centre of the case, and no-one wanted to miss a word of what he had to say. He began by confirming the items submitted for his examination, including materials which had been removed by the police from the King Henry Tavern. He then described the tests he had applied.

'I have no hesitation in declaring that the deceased ingested a fatal amount of strychnine,' he said. 'It is impossible to be exact about the quantity, but my best estimate based on the samples I examined is approximately one grain in total. I am unable to say in what form the fatal dose was taken. One possibility that has been suggested is that he might have taken one of the many tonic mixtures available and which are often consumed by athletes to stimulate the action of the heart and muscles. The amount of strychnine in these products are not, in normal use, harmful, and an excessive amount would have to be consumed to result in poisoning.'

'How much of, for example, Dr Wrothby's tonic would he have had to consume to receive a grain of strychnine?' asked the coroner.

'In excess of a full bottle,' said Russell. 'The stomach contents did show that apart from the strychnine, he had consumed both iron and quinine sulphate, which are common ingredients of such tonics, but not in any quantities likely to cause harm. The tonic is highly improbable as a cause of death, but I cannot entirely rule it out.

'Another suggestion has been made to me, with more serious implications, that Summers might have dosed himself with a harmless tonic mixture which had been adulterated with vermin destroyers of a kind sold by most chemists. These powders must be clearly labelled as poisonous and are dyed either with Prussian Blue or soot, to further warn the user that they are not to be consumed. I and my assistant have made the most strenuous efforts to discover any traces of dye or soot in the stomach contents of the deceased, without result. We are entirely satisfied that neither was present. I am therefore certain that Summers had not ingested any of the commonly available vermin powders.'

'Are there any such powders sold which are not dyed?' asked the coroner.

'Some chemists do formulate their own powders, and may unwisely neglect to add a dye, but the powders sold in all the chemists in the immediate area and the ones purchased for use at the King Henry were all dyed. In fact, to be quite certain of that, I dispatched my assistant to visit all the chemists in the neighbourhood and he confirmed that none of them sold an undyed powder.'

I realised that this energetic assistant must be Holmes. His account of working with Russell had suggested that he and the distinguished man had been almost equal partners in the investigation. He had not mentioned being sent out on errands. I glanced at him, but his face was like a statue.

'I was not presented with any evidence to show that anyone, either Summers or another person who might have had the opportunity of surreptitiously administering such a thing, had possession of an undyed vermin powder,' added Russell. He appeared to be looking at Sturridge as he spoke. The inspector was seated behind us. I did not turn to see his expression, tempting as it was to do so.

'Amongst the items submitted to me by the police, was a six-ounce bottle of Dr Wrothby's strengthening syrup, which was located in the lodgings of one of the boxers at the King Henry Tavern. Three ounces of the mixture remained. It was tested and found to contain very small quantities of strychnine. The formula is one sixty-fourth of a grain per drachm; that is one teaspoonful dose. I was also given three vermin killers formulated by Mr Fuller of Covent Garden. These are kept in the scullery of the Tavern. Their formula is very similar to Battle's, one and a half grains per powder, and they were dyed with Prussian Blue. All three packets were sealed and undamaged.'

'Did you,' asked the coroner, 'discover anything in the body fluids and organs of the deceased, other than the presence of strychnine, which might have accounted for his death?'

'I did not,' said Russell very firmly.

There were no further questions and Professor Russell returned to his seat.

Mrs Isabella Logan was next called to give evidence. Mrs Shem took her place with great self-assurance. She was carrying an account book under her arm and settled herself for the questioning by unfolding a pair of spectacles and perching them on her nose.

'Mrs Logan, please tell the court the nature of your occupation,' said the coroner.

'I am bookkeeper to the King Henry Tavern, and I also assist at the bar counter. My husband is the manager.'

'Are you able to advise the court of the purchases of vermin killers for use in the tavern?'

'I am.' She opened the volume. 'I record all purchases in our books. I also replenish our supplies of Fuller's vermin powders when there are none left in stock. The last use of our earlier stock of powders was in November. I used a whole powder, which I mixed with fat and put on pieces of bread. These I distributed in locations where only vermin might take them. I purchased three more from Fuller's chemists on 10 November. I have the slip here. They were stored in a box in our scullery. When the police took them away, none were missing.'

'These powders were dyed blue?'

'They were.'

'Have you ever purchased powders of this nature from another chemist?'

'No.'

The evidence was complete, and the coroner summed up and asked the jury to consider a verdict. The questions before them were not only determining the agent of the death but whether it had been administered by the deceased, and if so, with what intention, or by another hand. The verdicts open to them were suicide, misadventure, and murder. I noticed that manslaughter was not mentioned. If anyone had given Summers poison, it had to be assumed that it was done with the deliberate intention of causing harm.

The jurors decided to withdraw to another room for debate. Everyone else remained in their places. There were a few whispered conversations between individuals seated together, but there was no other sound apart from the rustling of papers and scratch of pencils.

I feared that we were to receive a verdict which would settle nothing and satisfy nobody, and so it proved. When the jury returned, they had been able to agree unanimously that Bill Summers had died as a result of poisoning with strychnine, but how and by whom this was administered and for what purpose it was impossible for them to decide.

I risked a glance at Inspector Sturridge. Clearly annoyed at the exposure of the flaws in his cherished theory, he rose abruptly from his seat and walked heavy-footed to address young Jones. In the face of Mr Stockdale, he was obliged to be courteous, but his intentions were obvious. Struggling to attempt a merely formal tone, he said that the police would continue to make enquiries to establish the truth, but strongly suggested that Jones should not think of leaving London for the present.

Once Sturridge had gone, taking his constables with him, Holmes had a kinder word with Jones and his father. Both were well aware that if the case could not be concluded to the satisfaction of the public, the suspicion of murder would always remain, and they feared that this might affect every aspect of the young boxer's future. Holmes promised to continue his efforts to get to the bottom of the mystery, but he looked troubled.

'Mrs Shem has given me a list of everything she knows was kept at the tavern and which might conceivably have caused the death of young Summers,' he said. 'All the vermin powders have been fully accounted for, and she is adamant that they did not purchase anything else which might have been a source of strychnine.'

'Might he have bought something himself before he came to London?' I suggested.

'Summers consumed stimulants because he was nervous of the match with Jones,' said Holmes. 'He was not nervous until Bowman's death and seeing the ebony idol, both of which events occurred after his arrival in London. Whatever he took was provided quite recently. Someone knows something about it and is keeping their silence, perhaps for reasons which have nothing to do with Summers's death. Whatever it is, I mean to find it out.'

CHAPTER THIRTY-TWO

It will not have escaped the notice of readers of this memoir, that in the closing weeks of 1876 Holmes was engaged in several enquiries simultaneously. It might be assumed from Watson's accounts of Holmes's later adventures, most of which were related in a brief and episodic manner, that he only undertook one investigation at a time. This was certainly true when cases were hard to come by, or the ones he was offered were declined as too commonplace to attract his attention. When he was a celebrated international detective, however, he was assailed by hosts of enquiries coming to his door and more urgent demands than time would allow. He often undertook several cases at once, dividing his energy between them, something which I believe led to the unwise reliance on stimulants, and breakdowns in his health which Watson chronicled.

Although the Bowman case had been quickly concluded and found not to involve a crime, it had acted like the mythical hydra, sprouting new heads as soon as one was cut off. Before long, Holmes had found himself with several enquiries, all likely to offer encouragement to the opponents of boxing and which he was therefore extremely anxious to resolve. While still pondering the unfathomable mysteries of the deaths of Bill Summers and Dr Wrothby, he had not abandoned trying to locate the missing boxer Lunn in order to discover the truth concerning the fight which had led to the death of Matthew Arroway.

Holmes had purchased a recent edition of *Fistiana: or the Oracle of the Ring*, a publication of the newspaper *Bell's Life in*

London and Sporting Chronicle, which listed boxers and their battles from 1700 to 1873. One afternoon, after some hours spent on my studies, I retired to the relative comfort of the students' common room, and found Holmes folded into an armchair, engrossed in the pages of *Fistiana.*

Not wanting to interrupt him, I took up a newspaper, but it was not long before he threw the book aside in frustration. 'It is hard,' he said, 'looking for a man whom no-one has seen in years, with no clue as to where he might be, no portrait of him and only a description which might apply to a thousand men in London alone. It is easy enough to find representations of the great figures of boxing, but Mr J. H. Lunn, while I have his height and weight, which chime with what Professor Logan told me, is only a minor figure. There is no record in *Fistiana* of his combat with Arroway, which is unsurprising as great efforts were made to conceal the fact that it happened at all. It lists his earlier bouts but nothing more recent of him.'

'Perhaps the rumour of his having gone to America is true,' I said. 'So many of the prize fighters have gone there.' I am sorry to say that this observation did not assist Holmes's mood. 'Or he might have died from drink,' I added, compounding my offence. 'He might have been found in the street and buried in a common grave, without being identified.'

To my surprise this thought seemed not to cause Holmes any concern; in fact, it rather improved his mood. His expression cleared and he sprang to his feet. 'Thank you, Stamford, you have unwittingly provided me with a useful line I will pursue.'

'Really?' I said, not entirely happy with the word 'unwittingly', although from Holmes any appreciation was something to savour. I had a horrid thought; I imagined Holmes prowling graveyards to find paupers' burials, and even

— no, that idea was too dreadful to allow to rest in my mind for even an instant. 'What are you planning to do?'

He gave a mischievous smile. 'That, for the moment, will remain my secret.'

Long before I enrolled as a student of surgery at Barts I acted as a surgical dresser, most notably for John Watson. I have witnessed numerous operations, and in the course of my subsequent training I watched and took part in many dissections of corpses and their organs. I have therefore seen for myself the effects of excessive drinking on the human anatomy. Despite this, I had never before this pugilistic case devoted serious thought to the evils of drink and the toll it took not only on the individuals going under the knife, but their families and society in general.

In the days that followed this conversation with Holmes, I thought of Lunn, who had quite probably destroyed himself and another man through drink. I thought of Bowman, whose career was in decline due to over-indulgence. Drink might not have played a part in his death, but had he prospered better his family might have been left without the need to appeal to charity. Robson, too, had once been a more robust figure, so I was told, but had found nightly consolation in the tavern after the death of his wife. I also wondered what dreadful things Dr Wrothby had done when he ought by rights to have been sober.

I was making my way to my humble rooms in Farringdon, where there were hostelries in plenty, offering good cheer to the working men in the neighbourhood, when I saw a sad figure in old rags, slumped against a wall, mumbling. A grimy bottle was clutched in one hand, which was bound about in a filthy bandage. I couldn't see his face, since a battered hat was pulled down over his eyes, and a tangle of unkempt hair protruded from under the brim. His age was unknowable, but he looked bony and frail, worn down by too little nourishment, supported only by the brief stimulus of what smelt to me like cheap spirits. I wondered if such a man had any home other than the street, and what chance there was that after a night spent unsheltered from the cold, the morning would find him mercifully released from his misery.

As I walked by, feeling helpless to do anything for his plight, one he shared with many hundreds of others in our prosperous capital, he turned towards me and grunted, holding out one hand, the palm cupped. It was clearly an appeal for money. I was of course, as students so often are, temporarily short of funds, especially as I had just purchased some volumes required for my studies. I knew that anything I gave him would only go to acquire more of the poison to which he was addicted, but who was I to deny a dying beggar the only comfort he knew in the world? I searched my pockets and found a shilling, which I dropped into his hand. He held up the coin to see what it was and uttered his gratitude in a tearful, broken voice.

I walked on towards my apartment, and something, I am not sure what, made me turn around to see what had become of him. I half expected to see him shuffling into the nearest tavern, or even sliding down the wall to the pavement in a state of collapse. Instead, he was walking away rather briskly, chuckling to himself. 'Holmes!' I exclaimed. 'That was my last shilling!'

I did feel a little aggrieved for a while and was obliged to apply to my parents for an advance on my allowance. I could not, however, fail to be impressed by Holmes's improved powers of disguise. I had once pointed out to him that to deceive those who knew him, it was imperative that he conceal both his unusual height and distinctive features, and he had done both. Holmes can be somewhat trying at times, but I was always even on the most difficult occasions proud to call him a friend.

Several days passed without sight or news of him, and once again I found myself concerned for Holmes's safety. If his appearance before me as an inebriated beggar was no random amusement, but an experiment to test his new disguise's effectiveness, then he must have been intending to make use of it, but how and where I did not know. I continued to haunt Barts daily in case a message had been left for me but received not a word. Some of the instructors were using the long vacation to work on their own studies, and one or two did enquire about Holmes, but I had nothing to tell them. I think they were, like myself, becoming used to his unexplained absences, only with far less reason to be worried.

The only person I could talk to on the subject was my friend George Luckhurst. By now he was aware that Holmes was currently engaged in following one of his cherished mysteries, although I was unable, due to the police investigation, to share any details. At university this pastime had aroused much undeserved derision amongst Holmes's fellow students. Those who lack his extraordinary brain power always tend towards hilarity in order to conceal their own deficiencies. Luckhurst is not and never was of that number.

He could see that I was fretting and tried to suggest a short excursion into the country to divert my mind from my worries, but soon realised that I wanted to remain available in London in case Holmes required my help. 'He has even been disguising himself,' I said. 'Who knows what desperate company he means to mix with?'

'False beard and wig, I suppose,' said Luckhurst. 'He did that occasionally to see if he could fool us. Of course, we all saw it through it.' He paused. 'Naturally that was because we knew him,' he added quickly. 'I am sure it would have been more successful with strangers.'

I was not to be consoled. Looking back on that time, as I write this memoir, I can understand the pain Watson so often felt when Holmes plunged into danger without his loyal companion by his side. I began to appreciate Watson's eagerness to pocket his trusty service revolver and accompany his friend into unknown perils. The good doctor's protracted agonies after the incident at the Reichenbach Falls are quite beyond my imagination. The blow must have blighted his happiness as much as or even more than the death of his wives. He was not alone in this. Strangers who had known neither man, but only read of their adventures, were seen wearing black armbands in mourning for the loss of a great hero and defender of the public safety. No wonder Watson fainted dead away from emotion when Holmes returned.

I am obliged to confess that I feel a certain amount of guilt that Watson was allowed to remain in ignorance of the true position for three years. There was a period when I was entrusted with Holmes's secret, and there are tales I can tell which must wait for another volume. I was granted this confidence, not because I was important, far from it — I was unimportant, that was my essential quality. My youthful adventures with Holmes had been kept from the public, partly because there were at the time, good reasons for secrecy, and partly because I had never considered writing a memoir until now. The cases Holmes solved together with Watson, on the other hand, had been published for anyone to read. Revealing what I knew about Holmes's activities during the years before his dramatic return might have placed his dearest friend and ally in grave danger. Holmes trusted me to remain silent, and I never betrayed that trust.

After an absence of a week, Holmes reappeared at Barts, as if nothing had happened, looking quite his old self, in excellent spirits, and apparently unaware of my anxiety for his safety. 'Come, Stamford,' he said, 'if you have nothing in hand, as I suspect you have not, we must go and have a meeting of some importance in this affair!'

'Who are we meeting?' I asked.

'The former pugilist and conqueror of Matthew Arroway, Mr J. H. Lunn.'

CHAPTER THIRTY-THREE

'You know where he is?'

'I do.'

'And does he know we are coming?'

'I hope not.'

'He might not wish to be identified.'

'I am sure of it.'

I decided I had best accompany Holmes, if only to save him from himself.

'Where are we going, Holmes?' I asked, concerned that we were about to enter some unwholesome and dangerous place, and wondering if we ought to have armed ourselves.

'The Christian Mission Hall, Shoreditch. If we walk smartly, we will be there in twenty minutes!'

We set off at a good pace, and I had to break into a trot now and then to keep up with Holmes's long-legged strides. 'Will Mrs Arroway be there? Or worse still, Miss Mitchell? It would be very unfortunate if they were to confront Mr Lunn.'

'I agree,' said Holmes with a smile, 'but according to the leaflet of which Mrs Goode granted me a brief sight, they are this afternoon addressing the inaugural meeting of the Ladies' Anti-pugilism League, and I expect Mrs Goode will be in attendance.'

I felt somewhat relieved. The Christian Mission, or as this organisation later came to be known, The Salvation Army, does valuable work amongst the poor, bringing the comfort of the gospel, as well as immediate relief from want. The Mission is especially devoted to the principles of temperance. So much misery is caused by husbands who have no sooner received their wages than they go into a tavern and pour it down their throats, not departing until all has been spent, leaving nothing for their wives and children. Wives, too, can become victims of excess, and what dreadful lives they must lead, to find refuge in oblivion. But no-one is beyond redemption, and all sinners are received and encouraged to find comfort in Christian fellowship. Lunn, once he had realised what he had done, might well have come to such a place.

As we walked, Holmes told me that he had used the disguise of a helpless but penitent drunkard to seek solace and hope at the Mission halls. He was given bread and tea and encouraged to pray. His sins, he was told, had already been forgiven. No-one disturbed his reflective contemplation, and he had been able to allow his powers of observation their full rein.

Our destination, a small new-built chapel house in warm red brick, had an inviting air. Anyone seeking comfort would naturally be drawn to its doors. Inside there was a generously sized hall, made especially attractive by arrangements of dried flowers and evergreens. The walls bore framed pictures of scenes from the Bible, and colourful banners painted with heartening quotations and cheerful mottoes. A harmonium stood ready to accompany the singing of hymns.

We entered upon a scene of cheerful industry. Long tables had been set out and covered in white cloths, with chairs set ready in expectation of a substantial throng. A host of ladies was busily loading the tables with all the necessaries for a substantial tea gathering. Every place was provided with a cup, saucer, plate, and spoon, and arranged down the centre of the boards were jugs of milk and basins of sugar. Platters were being brought, on which slices of buttered bread were stacked high like church towers, and there were hearty spiced loaves with glistening tops, ready to be cut, and baskets of warm, sweet rolls. A boiler had been set up in one corner, large enough to provide an ocean of tea for a hundred or more thirsty souls, and teapots were standing ready to convey supplies to the tables.

A lady was at the door, selling tickets. The charge was one shilling, and Holmes was decent enough to pay for me, which he did without comment.

The seats were very quickly being filled by a flood of eager arrivals. I looked about me and saw that the majority of those come for the gathering were ladies, many of whom had brought their children. I began to wonder if Mr Lunn would be in attendance, and if so, which of the few men he might be. I decided not to ask Holmes, as I felt sure he would take great delight in telling me nothing.

When we were in our places and it was time to start, a stooped, white-haired gentleman stepped forward and addressed us in a gentle voice, leading the company with a prayer to bless not only those present, but the tea, and offering thanks for the health of the founders of the Mission, Mr and Mrs Booth. Then the feast began. The boiler taps were opened, and teapots were filled to the brim and brought to the tables by a small army of waiting gentlemen in white aprons. I was informed by the lady beside me, who recognised that I was new to these events, that everyone working on the provision and delivery of the tea was a volunteer, happy to work for the good of the Mission. This generosity ensured that the ticket sales would raise funds for charitable works. She hinted to me that the waiters were all reformed sinners, by which I guessed she must have meant reformed drunkards.

Many of the ladies made short work of the generous provisions before them, which were as well-made as might be had in a teashop or a home where a good cook baked fresh every day. By the time I had cleared my plate, the opportunity of another helping had all but gone. The tea was hot and strong, and teapots were emptied and returned to be filled several times over. Holmes, I noticed, ate sparingly as he usually did, said nothing to anyone, simply nodded politely if spoken to, and looked pensively about him.

There was entertainment as well as conversation. The secretary, a portly fellow called Mr Harrison, rose to address us, and after fumbling with some papers and his spectacles, read out letters sent to the committee praising the work of the Mission in relieving poverty and fighting sin. Several individuals, flushed with the warmth of steam and company, rose to give personal testimony of how they had been rescued from the depths of despair and misery, and given hope of salvation, and a lady performed a song in praise of tea. The final event of the long afternoon was to ask the company to raise their voices in hymn-singing accompanied by the harmonium.

As the crowds departed, and the helpers united in tidying the hall and clearing away the last crumbs and crusts from the tables, Holmes rose from his seat and went to speak to the secretary.

'Mr Harrison, would you grant me some of your time for a private conversation?'

Harrison looked startled and looked at each of us in turn. 'If you wish to join our mission, you would both be very welcome,' he said.

'That is not the subject I wish to discuss,' said Holmes. 'It would be best for us to speak alone. Is there an office here we might use?'

'Is this a financial matter?' asked Harrison. 'Our treasurer —'

'No, it is not. I will be blunt with you, Mr Harrison. Or should I say, to give you your full name, Mr James Harrison Lunn, as printed in *Fistiana*.'

The man's face went quite white for a moment, and then I saw on his brow, what only Holmes must have detected, the faint scar of an old injury.

CHAPTER THIRTY-FOUR

Mr Lunn, for his expression showed it was he, was the picture of misery. To give him credit, he made no attempt to deny it.

'I always knew this moment would come,' he sighed. 'Are you the police?'

'No,' said Holmes, 'we are, however, acting for a lady who seeks to know the truth. Mrs Arroway.'

A sad smile flickered across his features. 'I will tell you what I can,' he said, 'but you will find that I hardly know the truth myself. Come this way. I will see that we are not disturbed.'

He spoke briefly to the elderly gentleman who nodded, then led us to a small side chapel where there was an alcove furnished with a row of devotional carvings and bench seats to assist contemplation. Lunn stared at the carvings for a while, then turned to us.

'Please believe me, I am not the man I once was,' he said. 'Drink was once my master, and an unkind master it is. It lures a man like the devil, with fine promises, but then when you are trapped in its claws, it shows its true nature. Of course, you want to know about the night I fought Matthew Arroway.'

We sat down. 'I was apprehensive,' Lunn began. 'He was young and strong and had something to prove. I thought one drink might calm me, help to manage my resolve, but then one drink became two, and well, I don't have to tell you how that turned out. Time passed and I knew I had to get to the Two Spires in time, or I might have had to pay a forfeit. I knew my way, even when under the influence. I think I must have stumbled, for later I found a cut on my head I could not remember receiving.' He laid his fingertips to his forehead.

'Like so many cuts of that nature, it bled rather freely and looked a great deal worse than it was. I remember a kind man helping me to my feet. I think I recall arriving at the tavern. But I have no memory whatsoever of the bout. The next thing I remember I was at home, and my sister, who I live with and is a veritable angel, was very upset at my condition, and a doctor was there.'

'Dr Wrothby?' asked Holmes.

'I see you know of him. Yes, he was seeing to my injuries. He told me what had happened.'

'Please tell us exactly what he said.'

Lunn briefly closed his eyes and took a moment to compose himself and order his memories. 'He told me that I had arrived at the Two Spires in an inebriated state, with blood running down my face. He had bound up the cut on my forehead. He thought I should not go on, but Meaney, he was the landlord, insisted that the fight must proceed, or he would have to repay the ticket price. So they plied me with coffee to try and sober me, and got me into the ring. It seems that Arroway, seeing my condition, was over-confident and let his guard down. I hit out and caught him so hard that he fell and struck his head. It must have been quite some blow because in doing so, I broke my wrist. Wrothby had to put it in a splint. Arroway was carried home in such a state that his life was despaired of. My sister wanted me taken to hospital, but Wrothby said I mustn't go, or questions would be asked, and if the truth came out, everyone concerned, including myself and Meaney might be arrested.'

Lunn pulled back his right sleeve and cuff. The scars of the injury were still apparent, and the wrist was misshapen. 'The break did not heal well, with the appearance you now see. I have some movement, but very little strength. I could not box again, of course, but then I no longer had an appetite for it.

However, I had already resolved to make a new man of myself. You see, I had found something in my pocket. The stranger who helped me after my fall had put a paper there about the work of the Christian Mission. I read it and could see my path laid out before me. But then I wondered, would the Mission really accept a wretch like me? I gathered my resolve, and dared go to a meeting, where I confessed what I had been, and wept like a child, and they welcomed me with joy in their hearts. From that day on, despite every temptation, despite the agony of craving, not a drop of alcoholic beverage has passed my lips. I became a member, and then an officer. I do a little work for them, and I preach the evils of drink. From what little money I can earn, I make sure to pay a portion to charity. My unusable arm is a blessing, in a way. It is a symbol of my message. I refer to it as the wages of my sin. But all this time I have had to live with the guilt of what I did, even though I have no memory of it.'

He paused and wiped his eyes with a handkerchief, overcome with emotion, and we allowed him to recover.

'There is something else I must confide. Some months ago, Mrs Arroway came to one of our meetings. I heard that her husband was never the same after that fight, and that he had recently died.'

'Mrs Arroway does not know your true identity?' asked Holmes.

He shook his head. 'No, and I dare not tell her. She is as good a creature as ever walked this earth. We have become friends. I wish —' He sighed. 'I wish to ask her to be my wife, and I know that if we were united, we would be happy. I would do everything in my power to ensure that. But if she was to discover my true name and what I once was and what I did, it could bring untold harm and great pain to us both.'

'I fear you may be correct,' said Holmes. 'But tell me, was the fight with Arroway arranged by Mr Meaney?'

'Yes, it was.'

'Did you not have a man who arranged your matches for you?'

He sighed again. 'I did once, but he refused to go on after I — well, it wasn't the first time I had arrived after drinking.'

'And Matthew Arroway? He was a promising young boxer. Did he not have a man to promote him?'

'No, but there was more than one man interested in him. That fight could have been his entry into greater things.'

'These men would have been there to see the fight?'

'Almost certainly. But I don't think you'll get them to talk about it. I wish they would. You see —' He gave a long pause. 'A short while ago, a curious thing occurred,' he went on. 'An officer of the Christian Mission who had been away founding a new centre in another town, returned to London, and when he saw me, he was overwhelmed with joy and greeted me as a brother, although I did not know him. Then he explained that he was the very man who had found me lying injured and inebriated in the street on that fateful day. It was he who had helped me up and put the paper in my pocket. He said that he had wanted to take me to a doctor, but I had told him that I had to be somewhere nearby very soon and that a doctor would be there, and he would look after me, so he allowed me to go on my way. He was of course delighted to see that I had found the peace of religion. And he enquired as to how my injuries had healed. The cut on my forehead, which still leaves a slight scar for those who choose to look for it, and my wrist. He asked me about the wrist, which he said he had noticed was almost certainly broken.'

'But Dr Wrothby said —' I exclaimed, 'and Shem Logan, he was the bartender who saw the fight. They both said that you broke your wrist when you hit Arroway.'

'Yes. I had always believed I had broken the wrist during the fight, but it now seems that it was broken before. And that led me to think. You see, it is my right wrist, and my stronger arm. I was known for the right to the jaw. My left — I have a stiffness in that shoulder, and it was nowhere near as strong. I would parry and feint with the left, then attack with the right.' Here Lunn looked at his right hand and gave a little sigh of regret for times past before he shook off the thought. 'How, I wondered, had I used a broken wrist to punch a man so hard that he fell, and not even remember it? All I can think is that Wrothby, seeing how it was when I arrived, bound up my wrist very tightly, and someone, either he or Meaney, put a stone in my left glove to give me the advantage, and told me to use my left. Of course, they are both dead, so I will never know the answer.'

Holmes had that determined look about him. 'I will find out the answer,' he said. 'I promise you that.'

'Will you? I want to know, even if it is not to my credit.'

Lunn turned his eyes towards the devotional carvings, bent his head and began to pray aloud. He prayed for release from his uncertainty, forgiveness for his sins, and the welfare of Mrs Arroway and her children. We joined him in those sentiments, and then left him to his contemplation.

'There is one man alive who will surely know what Wrothby and Meaney did that night,' Holmes said to me later.

'You mean Shem Logan? But he won't say, will he? He might be afraid he will be held responsible, even if he was acting under orders. And poor Lunn, I feel sorry for him. Can he really be blamed for what he did when drunk?'

'If drunkenness was a defence admissible in court, our prisons would not be as full as they are,' said Holmes. 'But he is less afraid of prison than losing the affection of Mrs Arroway. Still, I will do all I can for them both. I have a theory, but I am yet to devise a way of putting it to the test. If I am correct, then Mr Lunn will be able to propose to his lady with a clear conscience.'

CHAPTER THIRTY-FIVE

When I next watched Holmes sparring in the gymnasium with Professor Logan, I was able to see how his style had developed even over such a short time of instruction. No wonder Watson had been in awe of Holmes's martial skills; he had been trained by one of the best.

I too was making some progress. My exercise was not primarily for muscular development, and still less for proficiency in combat, but the maintenance of health and vigour. Cricketing practice in the summer kept me active, and I had found that sparring was an excellent alternative in the winter months. There was also an air of camaraderie, mutual respect, and encouragement amongst the boxing men, which I had come to appreciate.

Shem Logan did not spar, but he often came up to the gymnasium to replace towels and drinking water and replenish the buckets for our sponges. He moved slowly and quietly, carried out his tasks, and left. One hardly noticed he was there. I couldn't help wondering what secrets he might hold about the Arroway fight, but if he did, I could not see how anyone, even Holmes, would be able to extract them.

Once classes were over, Holmes told the professor that he would like to apprise him of his recent findings, and we went down to the office to speak privately.

We made ourselves comfortable, the professor wholly at his ease, while Holmes, leaning back in his chair, regarded him from narrowed eyes, like a cobra looking for a chance to strike.

'I continue to look for the origins of whatever poison killed Mr Summers,' said Holmes, 'but I have exhausted all possibilities except whatever is being kept a close secret. The vermin powders have been exonerated, and I do not believe that any other suspect product was ever purchased by the tavern. Both Wrothby's syrup and the pills made by Mr Fuller, some of which I have discovered were taken by Summers, are most unlikely to have caused his death. But I am sure that the fatal dose, whatever it was, was taken here.'

'The poison must have been given to him by another person,' said Logan.

Holmes did not comment on this, but continued, 'I am left with one conclusion, that there was another source of strychnine here that I know nothing about. Can you advise me about this?'

'I am sorry, but I can't.'

There was a troubled silence.

'On other matters,' said Holmes, smoothly, 'you might be interested to know that I was recently able to speak to the elusive Mrs Wrothby.'

'Oh,' said the professor.

'I am, of course, aware of the fact that she recently paid you a visit, a visit you took care to conceal from me.'

'Ah, well, there are some things it is best not to reveal where a married lady is concerned,' he said, with a grin. 'I have nothing to hide, but her new husband is a bit particular about where she goes and who she speaks to.'

'What was the reason for her visit?'

'Didn't she tell you?'

'She gave me her account; I would like to hear yours. I know it took place very soon after Summers's death, although she did not know about it at the time.'

'That is right. She had wanted to speak to me earlier, but found the place sealed off by the police and had to wait until they had gone. She had read in the papers about poor Bowman and wanted to know if there had been any suggestion that Wrothby's preparation had been involved in his death. She knew that Bowman used to take it.'

'What did you tell her?'

'I told her what you had said; that it looked very probable that the inquest would find that the tonic had nothing to do with it. She seemed satisfied with that.'

'You must have talked about Summers's death.'

'Of course.'

'The appearance of the body?'

'Yes. I said he looked like he had had some kind of seizure.'

'How did she respond to that news?'

'She was quite shocked by it. She said it was most unusual and upsetting for such a young man to die in that way. Then she asked if he had also taken Wrothby's syrup, and I was able to say that as far as we knew he did not. I mentioned that you were looking into it for me, and we hoped to have answers.'

Professor Logan continued to be comfortable with the conversation, and Holmes appeared satisfied with his replies. 'Did you also discuss the fight between Lunn and Arroway?'

'We did. She said, and this was the first I had known about it, that Wrothby had hinted that I might be involved in some way, and she was anxious to know if it was true, but I was able to reassure her that I had nothing to do with it. I was in Manchester that night, and I showed her the papers to prove it.'

'Did you have a wager on the fight?'

'I was tempted to bet on Lunn, but no, I was too busy with my own arrangements at the time.'

'Your brother might have placed a wager.'

'He doesn't usually bet. He didn't mention it, and I'm not about to ask him. I know that Shem helped Wrothby make Lunn fit to go into the ring, and he feels guilty over that, but I don't think he should. He only did what he was told to do both by Wrothby and Meaney.'

'When did Meaney die?'

'About two or three years ago. Liver. Swelled up and had to be tapped like one of his own barrels before he went. The Two Spires was sold off to pay his debts. I don't think any of the old crowd go there now.'

I wondered if Holmes had been to the Two Spires to make enquiries. I had the impression that Logan's comments did not surprise him but were simply confirmation of what he already knew.

'Prior to Mrs Wrothby's recent visit,' Holmes continued, 'when was the last time you saw her? Did she come here after the death of her first husband?'

'She was a single lady and could pay visits as she pleased,' said Logan with an unrepentant smile. 'Yes, she did. But some months after she was widowed, I think it was around Christmas that year, she told me that she had received a respectable offer of marriage, and that when a proper interval had passed, a wedding would take place. We decided that it would be best if she did not visit again. She would make a new life for herself in which our friendship would remain only as a memory.'

Holmes glanced at his notebook. 'Wrothby died in February 1873,' he said. 'This means that prior to her visit on the day of Summers's death, she had not been here for some three years.'

'Yes.'

'I understand that Wrothby treated her very ill.'

'He did. I don't think she ever told the half of it.'

'I have been reading the report of the inquest,' said Holmes. 'I know that Wrothby had a reputation for becoming aggressive when he was in liquor, but it was said that his manner on the night of his death was unusual. Can you tell me more about that?'

Professor Logan pondered this comment. 'Well, I'll tell you,' he said. 'Wrothby loved the boxing and all that went with it. He lived in that world, but he would never have been a fighter himself. A few drinks, though, and sometimes he imagined himself the great pugilist, ready to take on all comers, all weights. We humoured him, but no-one took it seriously. That night, yes, it was one of his quieter nights.'

'He never had fights here?'

'No, it was all talk with him, and we knew it.'

'Dr Goode said at the inquest that Wrothby had a lot of bruises on his body, most of which were old. It was suggested that he often staggered and hurt himself when intoxicated and bruised easily.'

'Oh yes, he used to bounce about in a sparring position and then he'd bump into a chair or table, and sometimes he fell over, and we had to pick him up and dust him down. I wasn't surprised when I heard about the bruises.'

'No one ever struck him?'

'Never that I was aware of.'

'Dr Goode mentioned that one of the bruises, one on the temple, was recent. Did Wrothby suffer a fall that night?'

'I didn't see any fall.'

'He was said to have been in a maudlin frame of mind.'

'Yes, he was in a strange mood. He started talking about things he had done in the past, and how some of them still preyed on him and he couldn't shake them off. He said —' Logan suddenly paused thoughtfully. 'Now, this was a new thing for him — something I had never heard him say before — he said he needed to be forgiven. I asked him for what and he just shook his head, but there were tears in his eyes. I put it down to drink. I did wonder, though, if the thing he most regretted was the cruel treatment of his wife.'

'You suggested he go home?'

'Yes, I thought a night's sleep in his own bed would put him right. He wasn't too steady on his feet, so I guided him to the door of the coach yard and said he should go home and rest and all would be well in the morning.'

'Did you see any marks on him then? None on his face?'

'Not that I remember.'

'You didn't see him drive away?'

'No, that was the last I saw of him. Robson saw he was bad, so he went out to help him into the chaise.'

'Robson must have been drinking too, that night.'

'He was, of course, he always did, but when he came back in, I thought he looked sober enough. He said to me, "I told Wrothby that the Almighty would forgive him his sins, and then I put him in the chaise. He's off home, now."'

'And the barmaid, Annie, she saw him sitting in the chaise and driving out of the coach yard?'

'Yes.'

'Was he in a fit state to drive?'

'If he wasn't, the horse was.' Logan shrugged. 'Maybe he fell out on the way home and got back in, and that was what made the mark you mentioned.'

There was nothing more the professor could tell us and as we left the tavern, Holmes was singularly pensive. 'Dr Wrothby, for all that he was tolerated for his services to boxing, was otherwise a most unpopular man, and his demise was regretted by no-one. His death is uniformly accepted to be from natural causes, all the bruises to be the result of accidents, and everyone is quite satisfied with that.'

'Are you satisfied, Holmes?'

'No, I am not.'

CHAPTER THIRTY-SIX

The noise in a crowded tavern is substantial, but nothing produced by the human voice, even when well lubricated by beer, can match that in a well-attended gymnasium when Professor Logan has decided to give a display of sparring with one of his young protégés. The event I was privileged to witness began as quite an informal affair, developing from one of the regular lessons, but the young pretender was too eager to show off his talents, imagining that he was ready to play teacher to his instructor.

Gradually, all the men became aware that this was no longer a lesson, or even a display, but a match. Everyone stopped what they were doing and gathered about the ring to watch the master of his art at work. Walter Robson looked on with satisfied appreciation of the man he had once trained, chuckling occasionally, when, I suspected, he recognised moves that he had taught. Harry Baxter was there, and he studied the young opponent with professional interest. Even Shem Logan, who was about to return to the bar, put down his bucket and stopped to watch his brother.

Professor Logan never sought to humiliate his students, but he was a strict teacher and made them work hard, showing not only his muscular strength and considerable experience but the intelligence and accuracy of his work. After a while, the youth, who was probably about my age, began to tire. His movements slowed, while his breaths were faster, and his punches were less accurate. Logan, although older, was in disciplined control, knowing how to make the most of his energy instead of spending it too freely at the start. While both men were sweating, the professor looked fresher.

A few of the youth's friends were cheering him on, hoping that their voices would rouse him to greater efforts, but most of us were applauding the professor. There was a brief rest for them both, and Shem was about to step up to assist, but the youth shook his head and wryly admitted defeat. The two men came to the centre of the ring and shook gloved hands while the room rang with thunderous appreciation. Shem brought wet sponges, towels, and drinking water, and as the professor stepped from the ring, he laughed, stripped off his sweat-soaked shirt and tossed it aside.

It was only then, when all eyes were on him, and the noise had faded from a roar to a babble, that anyone noticed that the gymnasium had been invaded by the angry ranks of the Ladies' Anti-pugilism League. Six ladies in brightly coloured silk sashes, carrying posters and banners denouncing pugilism and demanding that it should be made unlawful, were ranged against the men of the boxing club. There were sharp intakes of breath from every direction.

Had Professor Logan been a gentleman, he might have thrown a towel across his glistening torso, but he was no gentleman. He smiled at the new arrivals, and with every indication of politeness, approached the deputation which was led by a particularly belligerent Miss Mitchell. A few of the ladies seemed inclined to draw back to keep their distance, but Miss Mitchell boldly stood her ground. Her friends wavered but did not desert her. I recalled what Mrs Shem had told us of Miss Mitchell, her former association with boxing in the shape of the redoubtable Butcher Blunt, who had once been her intended. This and her iron will must have enabled her to prepare her companions for the sights they might expect in a gymnasium. All the deputation looked solidly determined not to show fear, or to be moved by the display of handsome masculinity before them. 'Good afternoon, ladies. Is there anything I can do for you?' said the professor.

'We want answers to our questions!' exclaimed Miss Mitchell. 'Answers about Matthew Arroway!' Her friends nodded emphatically, and murmured assent.

'I wish I could tell you what you want to know,' he replied, 'but you must all be aware that I had nothing to do with that sad event and know nothing of how it came about. The men believed to be responsible have already gone to beg forgiveness from their maker. Can you not be content with that?'

'All we are told is lies!' retorted Miss Mitchell. 'A guilty man is still being protected, and the blame is put on this man Lunn, a drunken creature who might never have been there, and wouldn't know it if he was. You, sir —' and here she stabbed an accusing finger at the professor — 'are a brute and a murderer. We know that you are capable of killing with a single blow. We think that you were the one who struck Matthew Arroway. Confess it now!'

'I am a brute, I admit it,' said Professor Logan, mildly. 'But I am no murderer.'

'If I may be allowed to intervene,' said Holmes. 'Miss Mitchell, there is abundant evidence that Professor Logan was not in London on the day of the Lunn and Arroway match. He was fighting a bout in Manchester that evening, and he could not have returned to London in time. There are too many witnesses to be denied.'

Miss Mitchell was not pacified. Instead, she turned her fury towards Holmes. 'We asked you to discover the truth, which you promised to do. Not only have you failed to make good your promise, but we now find that you have sided with these monsters. Shame on you!'

'I am on the side of truth,' said Holmes, 'whatever and wherever it might be.'

'Then tell us all now, what is the truth? Reveal it to the world, why don't you! Who killed Matthew Arroway? Name the man!'

Holmes paused. He looked around the gymnasium at the watching assembly, all waiting for his words. 'I regret that I do not have the answer,' he said at last. 'Whether it will emerge in time, I cannot say.'

Miss Mitchell uttered a snort of frustration and gave Logan a look that would have speared most men to the floor, then shook her fist at him. 'I wish I was a man!' she exclaimed.

He favoured her with a rather curious smile. 'I am very glad that you are not,' he replied.

She scowled. 'You have not heard the last of this! We are many and we are strong! We will prevail!' Mustering her ladies, she urged them from the gymnasium.

'Back to work, men!' said Logan before anyone had something to say. 'And remember, we offer courtesy and a strong supporting arm to the ladies. A worthy lady won with kindness is won forever.' There were mutterings amongst the boxers, but they did as they were told.

'Holmes,' I said, 'I notice you did not make your customary pledge of success to Miss Mitchell. Do you think that Arroway's death is a mystery you can't solve?'

'Far from it,' said Holmes. 'I have every confidence that I can. I may have addressed Miss Mitchell just now, but my words were actually intended for every person in the room. She does not know it, but her incursion has been of great assistance to me. I watched the reactions to her words, and to mine, and I now see a way of flushing out the truth. I have plans to put in place before I can act, but I feel that I am very close to a solution.'

CHAPTER THIRTY-SEVEN

'Sometimes,' said Holmes, 'the smallest indications, when one assembles them correctly, lead to a clear picture, and thus to the truth. They might not constitute absolute demonstrable proof, such as might convince a jury. They might be a mere collection of circumstances, a glance, a way of speaking, even what an individual chooses not to say, but slight as they are, I observe them, and together they tell me all. It only remains to reveal to my suspect that I know the truth and indicate that further dissembling is futile, in order to achieve a confession.'

'I would welcome it if you would reveal your train of thought,' I said. 'I shall never be able to solve mysteries as you do, Holmes, but I do try to understand how you come to your conclusions.'

Some days had passed, and we were in a small tavern near Barts where Holmes could indulge in his habit of tobacco. He was even in those days developing the skill which astonished Watson, and indeed, Watson's readers, when faced with an apparently insoluble mystery he would retire to an armchair with his pipe and submit the problem to the workings of his unique mind, emerging some while later with a fully developed solution. I do not know if it was the stimulus of the weed itself, the flavour, the inhalation of the smoke or just the action of rhythmic puffing at the pipe, which, so Holmes claimed, helped him solve the most baffling of mysteries. I was not about to plunge myself into the habit to find out.

'The questions I have been asking myself,' said Holmes, 'are where did Summers obtain the poison that killed him, what form did it take, and how and by whom it was administered.'

'And you believe you know the answer?'

'I do. It began,' he said, 'with something Mrs Goode said. After the death of her first husband, Dr Wrothby, she had sold the rights to produce the tonic mixture labelled with his name and had no further wish to advertise anything connected with him. Prior to her second marriage, she was employed as housekeeper to Dr Goode, who told her that if asked she should recommend the products sold under his label. We also know that in the early days of her widowhood, she paid visits to the King Henry. Whether Dr Goode knew of these assignations, I very much doubt. Once she saw the prospect of an advantageous marriage, however, she could not risk continuing those visits. The last one would have been about three years ago.

'We know that the tavern did not supply medicinal products for the boxers, other than those for external application. During the lifetime of Dr Wrothby, his wife had delivered supplies of his liniments to the tavern. When the boxers wanted a tonic mixture, they purchased their own and remained loyal to Wrothby's. None of Dr Goode's products were found anywhere in the tavern, and none were received by Barts for analysis.

'I did wonder, however, might Mrs Wrothby, when housekeeper to Dr Goode, take samples of his products to the tavern? If her clandestine visits had been discovered, she could then claim they had an innocent purpose. I made enquiries and learned that in the autumn of 1873, Dr Goode had just begun to produce the products sold under his name and was eager to make them known. There was Dr Goode's Superior Strengthening Syrup, recommended to sportsmen to act on the muscles, especially those of the heart, and Dr Goode's Superior Strengthening Pills, sold in boxes of a dozen.'

'But if she had taken any of these to the tavern,' I said, 'it would have been three years ago.'

'Precisely,' said Holmes. 'In considering what poisons were available, both we and the police have only thought of recently acquired materials, and those which were purchased and of which there would be some record. We have no note, no evidence, of samples provided gratis. Do you recall Mrs Goode's expression when she told us she was asked to recommend Dr Goode's products? Something was troubling her, something she did not reveal. I decided to test my theory. It was necessary for me to appear once again in the guise of Mr Sherrinford, and I invited Miss Sally to join me in a pot of tea and a plate of buns. Everyone has their price, Stamford, it is merely a matter of knowing it.

'Sally spoke freely about the visits made to the tavern by the newly widowed Mrs Wrothby. I asked her about the last time Mrs Wrothby visited under her own name, prior to her arrival as Mrs Taylor. Sally confirmed that there was indeed a passage of time of some three years. She recalled the visit during the Christmas season of 1873, and on that occasion, Mrs Wrothby had brought a package with her, wrapped in paper, and tied in string. This she handed to the barmaid, Annie, saying only that it was for the tavern. Annie opened it. There was a bottle of mixture which Annie said the boxers wouldn't want, as they preferred Wrothby's, but she thought her grandmother might like it, as she was under the weather and needed a tonic, and she took it away with her. But there was something else — a small, round box, which Annie didn't take away. Sally never saw what was in it or where it went. It wasn't put in the kitchen or the scullery. Neither was it in the medicine cabinet in the gymnasium. Sally cleans regularly and is quite sure of that. It was not in the tavern when the police made their search after

Summers's death. But I believe that at some time in the last three years a source of strychnine, which we had not previously suspected, and which can only have been a box of Dr Goode's pills, was in the tavern, quite possibly in Annie's possession.'

'Who else would have known it was there?' I asked.

'It is impossible to say for certain. But we already know that before Annie left to marry, she and Mary had shared a bedroom, and were on good terms.'

'Have you analysed Goode's pills?'

'I have. I purchased a box and compared them with other products. The pills made by Mr Fuller contain one sixty-fourth of a grain of strychnine, and he recommends a dose of one or two. There are other pills on sale which are twice as potent as Fuller's, and these also consider two pills to be a safe dose. Dr Goode's superior pills are four times as potent, and he recommends a dose of just one pill per day, the maximum amount doctors recommend, with a warning not to exceed that amount. And my examination of the material of the box under the microscope shows that its composition is very similar to the fragment I found in Summers's room.'

'If Summers had found those pills, he might not have realised that they were so much stronger than Wrothby's,' I said. 'And we know that he was in the habit of taking more than the stated dose of those.'

'Yes, he might even have mistaken the initial symptoms of poisoning to be nervousness and taken more. Six would have made him very ill indeed, and the whole box — I think we saw the result.'

'But how did he get them? He didn't know where they were, did he?'

'I don't believe he knew, but Mary certainly could have. She might have found the box of Goode's pills in her lodgings where Annie had put them, or even been given them by Annie. She had seen how worried Summers was, and she had already bought Fuller's pills for him and seen him take them several at a time without coming to any harm. She might have suggested to Summers that he try Goode's pills. Superior strengthening — it must have sounded just the thing. She isn't to blame. She meant to help.'

I gave some thought to Holmes's reasoning and could detect no obvious flaw. It was all supposition, but none of it was impossible. 'If you are right, then Mary is too frightened to say anything. What can we do?'

'I have already put plans into effect. I have asked Mrs Shem to speak to the girl, explain to her that we know what has happened and make it clear that we attach no blame to her. She must also be made to understand that if she does not speak up, then an innocent man might be charged with murder. I am pleased to say that Mrs Shem knew at once what to do and how she might set about it. I hope that that will be all that is needed.'

Holmes returned to his pipe.

Mrs Shem was as good as her word, and Holmes's judgement proved to be correct. Only that lady's gentle and intelligent approach could have brought the truth from the unhappy girl and given her the strength she needed to tell what she knew. Mrs Shem wrapped her trembling charge in a warm cloak and took her in a carriage to Scotland Yard to make a statement, insisting that she be allowed to sit by her side throughout in silent support. They were promised that the new information would be passed to the coroner, and we awaited a fresh determination.

I was relieved to hear in due course that Mary was not to be charged with any crime, but understandably she did not feel able to return to her work at the King Henry, where she felt sure she would still encounter some blame. She had been a diligent employee, and Mrs Shem recommended her to a good position in another establishment.

A few days later, Sergeant Lestrade brought us the good news that it had been accepted that Summers's death was the result of misadventure. Holmes ought to have been triumphant but when he sought me out in the college library to let me know, and we repaired to the common room to talk, he passed off the success as something quite simple. He remained quietly thoughtful, but at last he turned to me, and said, 'I have received a note from the King Henry. The Logans will entertain a small party tomorrow night to celebrate Jim Jones's exoneration. We must both attend.'

'I would be delighted,' I said.

'And I must warn you that I am about to do something that might prove to be dangerous.'

'Is that wise?' I exclaimed, realising that whatever the plan, it was futile to try and dissuade him.

He directed one of his firmer looks at me. 'And I require an accomplice!'

I could do nothing other than agree to help, as I felt sure that Holmes would be in even more danger if I was not there.

'Perhaps you could also ask a policeman to accompany us?' I suggested. 'I am sure Lestrade would make himself available.'

He shook his head. 'Lestrade is all very well in some situations, but if a police presence was detected then my scheme might come to nothing.'

'What do you want me to do?'

'I will make the preparations and when they are complete, I will provide you with instructions,' said Holmes. He gave me no indication as to what he was planning, but every now and then he gave a little chuckle to himself, and I knew that did not bode well.

CHAPTER THIRTY-EIGHT

The following evening, a festive assembly, which included the Logans, Walter Robson, Jim Jones, his father, and Mr Stockdale, was gathered at the King Henry. It was after the evening classes had ended, and we made a hearty dinner around the table in the basement kitchen, with foaming jugs of beer fresh from the barrel.

Jones was remarkably quiet during the meal, and his father and lawyer did most of the talking. There was naturally some speculation about Jones's future. Many boxing men in the intervals between matches find well-paid employment as bodyguards for wealthy men, but when this was mentioned, Jones made it clear that he did not intend to do this. It was too like the life of servitude he wished to avoid. He wanted to be his own man.

'I know that this business was not the public attention you had hoped for,' said Professor Logan, 'but your name is known now, and I think everyone will want to see you. Harry Baxter is still in London; he's up at the Piccadilly Tavern tonight, arranging some of the biggest matches of his career, and he'll be back here tomorrow. He's sure to have a word.'

Jones senior glanced at his son, who smiled a little before he replied. 'I have decided to return to Cornwall,' he said. 'I have not yet taken a decision about my future, and I think that spending some time with my family in Truro will help me to resolve my thoughts. There is also a young lady there, and I need to ask her if she would prefer being married to a boxer or a metalsmith.'

Mrs Shem said nothing, but she gave an affectionate glance at her husband. I could see from her expression what her preference would be.

The hour was growing late, and Jim Jones and his party said their farewells and returned to their hotel. The remaining company stayed on and once the dishes were cleared, there was still beer to be had and toasts to be drunk. I thought that Holmes looked unusually merry under the influence of alcohol, but I was obliged to decline further drinks and give notice of my imminent departure, saying that I had promised to spend the remainder of the evening with my parents who had family guests. Holmes, rather than return to his lodgings, and looking a little unsteady on his feet, asked if he might stay the night at the tavern, using the room recently vacated by Jones, and this was agreed.

'I have business to undertake tomorrow and must be well rested,' he announced. 'You recall that Miss Mitchell demanded of me recently that I discover the secrets behind the death of Matthew Arroway. I was unable to do so at the time, but she was most insistent, and for the sake of the widow, and her future happiness, I have been pursuing my enquiries with fresh energy. I have a meeting arranged for tomorrow morning, and I am confident that this will at last provide the final piece of information I require to complete my investigation.'

I made my farewells to the company, and headed up the basement stairs, but instead of leaving the tavern, I continued up, as Holmes had earlier instructed me, and went to lodging room three where we had agreed to meet. Not long afterwards, Holmes, who I knew had only made a pretence of inebriation, joined me.

The room was chilly as no fire had been lit, but it had been dusted and the bed made up. Holmes lit the gas.

'Are we to sit up all night?' I asked, shivering a little. Holmes was wearing his warm ulster and, in any case, always seemed impervious to weather of any kind.

'I think we have a little time before matters develop,' said Holmes. 'But you will have a warm bed for now.' He threw back the lid of the large blanket box which contained only laundered bedclothes and a spare pillow. 'There, Stamford, try that for size.'

I stared at it. 'You want me to sleep in there?'

'Not sleep, I hope, but you are of a height to be comfortable in so small a space, which is not the case with me, and I will ensure that there will be enough gaps for air. Make sure that you keep your limbs properly exercised so if I should happen to require you, it will take only moments for you to emerge. Oh, and place your watch under the pillow, or the ticking might give you away. Your presence must not be detected. I expect to receive a visitor tonight and the conversation should be extremely interesting. Your task will be to listen and remember what you hear.'

'Who are you expecting?'

'The person who will tell me all that there is to know about the night of the Lunn and Arroway fight. The facts that have not yet been made public.'

He stood expectantly by the chest and rather reluctantly I climbed in and found the most comfortable position possible. The linens and blankets did at least ensure that I would be warm, and I was even able to tuck the pillow under my head. Holmes placed some folded handkerchiefs between the body of the chest and the lid, providing both gaps for air and a space to press my ear for my vigil. It was not the most pleasant position, but had I been taller it would have been impossible. It was one of those rare occasions when I was able to assist Holmes in a manner which was beyond the capabilities of John Watson.

I peered through the gap and for a while saw Holmes moving about the room, then he extinguished the gas. I heard the soft sound of bedclothes being arranged, and finally all was quiet.

I don't know how much time passed. The curtains had been drawn close and there was very little light piercing the room either from streetlamps or the moon. As my eyes gradually became accustomed to the near dark, I looked out again but saw only the bed with the shape of Holmes's figure under the covers. Was he really so careless as to sleep, or was he merely pretending to be asleep to put any visitor off his guard? I flexed my knees, thankful for the recent sparring practice which had added some agility to my limbs. I heard through the wood and the bedding the usual sounds of people moving about, making their way to their rooms for the night, footsteps pressing softly on carpets, low voices, and then all was quiet for a time. In room number three, there was not a sound.

Then after a long silence, I heard something new. Footsteps, which I thought proceeded from the stairs, someone shuffling rather than stepping as if trying to conceal their approach. I held my breath, hoping that the sound would move past our door, wondering if perhaps it was no more than someone going to bed late after making the kitchen tidy or locking up the premises. But the steps halted outside our door. I heard the rasp of a match. Whoever it was must have been looking at the number on the door to make certain of finding the right one. Then, the handle turned very quietly, and a figure entered and approached the bed.

I am not sure quite what I expected to happen. Holmes had said he was anticipating a conversation with a visitor, and I suppose I expected the arrival to whisper to him and shake him awake. But he did neither of those things. He drew something from a pocket, lifted it high in the air and began to rain heavy blows on the head of the sleeping man.

CHAPTER THIRTY-NINE

I do not know what demon can have possessed me as I heard the sickening thumps and imagined my friend's skull crushed and bleeding under the weight of some heavy weapon. I threw back the lid of the chest, sprang out, and with a strangled shriek, propelled myself at the murderous shadow. It was not courage, I would never pretend that; it was desperation, hysteria, and a mad, blind carelessness as to consequences. I had never known the urge to kill before that moment, and I hope never to feel it again.

The intruder, startled by the fall of the lid, paused, turning in the direction of the noise. I saw only a dark shape, one arm held high, grasping some horrible object. Moments later I crashed wildly into him, and more by good fortune than skill, managed to seize his wrist with both hands. He was strong, most certainly stronger than I, but the weight of the collision and success of my grasp bore him over onto the bed, and there we struggled, briefly, before rolling bodily to the floor, the only sounds uttered being gasps and grunts. I think I managed a half sobbing cry for help. I wriggled like a fish, but next moment his solid heavy body was on top of me, bearing me down. His free hand circled one of my wrists with crushing strength and began to wrench my grasp from his arm. I was an instant away from utter helplessness. Then to my astonishment, a calm voice said, 'Keep still, and drop your weapon. I have a gun pointed at your head and I will use it if I have to.'

It was Holmes. How he was alive and unhurt I could not fathom, but it was enough that he was.

Our intruder did the sensible thing, and I heard the cudgel drop.

'Face down!' snapped Holmes. I was finally free from the weight pinning me down, and a shuffling sound suggested compliance. A coiled rope was thrust into my hands. 'Stamford, make our prisoner secure. You have nothing to fear. If he tries anything, I will shoot him.'

The curtains were drawn back, and I saw silhouetted against the moonlit sky Holmes's noble profile and the shape of his hand holding a gun.

I was shaking so hard I could scarcely hold the rope, but I did my best, crawling onto my knees beside the prone figure, pulling together the thick arms and tying the wrists as well as I could. Holmes, pocketing the gun, tested my pathetic attempts at knots and tightened them, speedily adding further loops of rope, so leaving his attacker lying trussed like a bundle of old clothing on the rug.

'Are you hurt, Stamford?' he asked in a surprisingly gentle tone.

I sniffled. 'I — no — that is, I don't think so. Holmes — are you — I feared —'

'I was behind the coat stand,' he said.

Relief is a powerful and exhausting emotion, and I briefly allowed it to overwhelm me. I am not sure Holmes even knew how to deal with it in another person. 'Stout fellow,' he said, with an embarrassed cough. 'You did well.'

I had no need to ask Holmes if he would have shot the intruder; I had no doubt of it. The gun was all too familiar. It had once been in the hand of a murderer and pointed at me.

The noise of the scuffle had by now wakened several of the occupants of the tavern. The door was flung open, and I saw an assembly of persons standing in the corridor, some bearing lit candles, staring into the room, their faces looking like ghosts in the flickering light. Shem and Mrs Shem stood side by side, in their nightshirts, clasping hands and looking afraid. Professor Logan wore only his drawers, while Rose was wrapped in his flannel dressing gown. Cowering behind them was Tilda, with a shawl thrown over her nightgown.

'What's happened?' demanded Logan, striding into the room. 'Who is this?'

'Attempted murder,' said Holmes, as the professor's candle flame revealed the features of our intruder, Mr Harry Baxter.

Logan looked about the room, the gnarled club that had dropped to the floor, the bed in which Holmes had placed a rolled blanket, and the savagely crushed turnip that lay on the pillow. He turned to the others. 'Bella, you look after Rose. Tilda, get dressed and go and get a policeman, and see he has another one with him.' Tilda scampered away.

Baxter struggled to sit up. 'Look, Calum, we can talk about this, we can come to some agreement,' he said. 'No-one wants the truth to come out.'

'About time it did,' said Logan with an oath. 'Now, you keep still and shut your mouth, or I'll shut it for you.' Baxter, who was probably as frightened of Logan's fists as he was of Holmes's gun, did as he was told.

'Shem, stand guard over this fellow while I get dressed,' said Logan to his brother, who was still standing uncertainly in the corridor.

'I would be grateful if Mr Shem could first bring a draught of brandy for Stamford, who has had something of a fright,' said

Holmes. 'I do not think Dr Wrothby's syrup would be of use here.'

Holmes helped me up from the floor so I could sit on the bed. I think I might have whimpered. Logan nodded at Shem, who went to get the brandy.

When Holmes lit the gas, I saw his heavy ulster hanging on the coat stand. It was only later I appreciated that after arranging the bed to make it appear that he was sleeping there, he had been able to conceal himself behind the voluminous garment in whose pockets he had carried all the necessaries for the adventure. I am not sure I ever entirely forgave him for the horrible experience of that night. He had his own ways of making up for his often cavalier treatment of his friends, but these did not usually amount to an actual apology.

The professor stayed with us to ensure that Baxter did not attempt to escape, while we waited for the police.

'What I don't understand,' said Logan, 'was how Baxter got in? He was over at the Piccadilly, and our doors were all locked. And who was he expecting to find in this room? Jones?'

Baxter said nothing.

'He was expecting to find me,' said Holmes. 'And he came in because he was let in. Do you see his boots?'

Logan inspected Baxter's boots, which bore traces of red mud on the soles. 'Yes, Mrs Shem won't be happy with that. Look at that mud. Where did that come from?'

'There are some repairs to the roads being carried out not far from here,' said Holmes. 'I collected some of the red mud, which was very distinctive, and shortly before I entered I smeared it outside the front and back doors of the tavern. Baxter stepped in it as he arrived.'

At that moment, Shem arrived with my brandy. 'And here,' said Holmes, 'is the man who let him in.' We looked at Shem Logan's boots into which he had thrust his bare feet, before going downstairs to the bar, and saw the same red mud clinging to them.

CHAPTER FORTY

'Shem?' exclaimed his brother.

Shem hesitated, looking at Holmes's confident stare with growing alarm.

'Now, don't run off,' said Logan. 'Come in and sit down. I want to talk to you.'

Reluctantly, Shem obeyed. Logan put down the lid of the blanket box so they could sit side by side.

'What's all this with you letting Baxter in here to attack Mr Holmes?' asked the professor. 'The truth, now. You've got the same mud on your boots as he has, so we know you've been out tonight.'

I never did get that brandy, because Shem impulsively tossed the entire glass-full down his throat. 'I didn't know he was going to do that!' he said. 'He said he was just going to talk and come to some arrangement.'

'Mr Baxter has his own ideas about arrangements,' said Holmes. 'I have long suspected that you knew more than you were saying, but the question was, how were we to learn it? When Miss Mitchell led her ladies into the gymnasium demanding answers about the death of Matthew Arroway, I was able to observe the reactions of those about me, and I saw you and Baxter exchange significant looks. I already knew that you were at the Two Spires on the night of the fight with Lunn, but in that moment, I felt sure that he was there, too, his business being to watch a promising prospect. I said that I was unable to help Miss Mitchell because I needed time to arrange a trap, and it would not do to attract attention too early. Tonight, my plan was in place. I gave an appearance of being inebriated and asked to stay here overnight after announcing to all present that the solution would be in my hands the next day. I selected room number three because it was the only one where there were places of concealment for both Stamford and me. Baxter was at the Piccadilly Tavern only a short distance away, and you went to warn him that you were both about to be exposed. He must have told you he would come here for a private conversation with me. I do, however, accept your explanation that you did not realise he intended to silence me in a more permanent manner.'

Shem hung his head.

'But Shem hasn't committed a crime!' said Logan. 'Whatever he did at that fight, he did under the orders of his employer. No court would ever convict him. And tonight, he did nothing against the law.'

'I do not intend to give him into custody,' said Holmes. 'If he ever comes to court, it will be because of his own confession.'

'I don't understand,' said Logan. 'He has nothing to confess.'

At that moment, Mrs Shem returned to the room and without a word handed Logan his dressing gown, which he put on. 'Tilda's gone for the police,' she said. 'There's a man on point very near, so they shouldn't be long.' She looked at her husband. 'Shem, are you well?'

He rubbed his eyes. 'Yes, Bella, please go back to bed. I'll wait here until the police have come.'

She looked around at us, reading our expressions. She knew there was something dreadfully amiss, beyond what obvious, but must have realised that she was not about to learn it then. 'We can talk later,' she said, and left us.

Two constables arrived soon afterwards, and after hearing and making a note of Holmes's account of the incident, they inspected the room and removed Mr Baxter, his club, and the broken turnip.

'Shem,' said Logan, 'we know the part you played at the Two Spires, but you can't go on blaming yourself. You weren't the man in charge. Now, let's all go back to our beds.'

'Not yet,' said Holmes. 'It is time the whole truth was known.'

Logan had been rising to his feet, but he paused at the quiet assurance of Holmes's voice. He sat down. 'All right,' he said. 'If there's more, let's have it.'

'I was able to talk to Mr Lunn recently,' said Holmes. 'He is neither dead from drink nor in America. But he had an interesting tale to tell.'

Logan glanced at Shem, who had leaned forward, wrapping both arms about his head so we could not see his face. 'Go on,' he said.

'He has no memory of his fight with Matthew Arroway. In fact, he barely recalls arriving at the Two Spires. We know that he had a fall on the way and cut his forehead, which was bleeding. We also know that he had a broken wrist, his right wrist.'

'Yes, he did that when he hit Arroway,' said Logan.

'He did not,' said Holmes. 'He has recently discovered from the man who helped him up after his fall that the broken wrist was also a result of that accident. When Lunn arrived at the Two Spires, he was quite unfit to compete at all. He was wondering if he was put into the ring with his left glove illegally loaded.'

'I wouldn't put it past Meaney to do that,' said Logan. 'Shem, was that what happened?'

Shem sat up a little and shook his head. 'But you're right, Mr Holmes. When Lunn arrived, he was drunk and the cut on his head was bleeding all down his face. Dr Wrothby bound up the cut, and Meaney told me to make coffee to help sober the man, so I did that, and when we tried to give it to him, we saw that his wrist was broken. Meaney was beside himself, because he knew the man couldn't fight, and he would lose money.'

'Meaney had to find some way of the bout going ahead,' said Holmes. 'I think his solution was to substitute another man. Perhaps it was Baxter's idea, I don't know. There was no other boxer present who might have stood in for Lunn convincingly, but there was one man there with some knowledge of the ring, who was the same height and build as Lunn. Shem Logan.'

'Oh no,' said the professor, 'that can't be. They are of a size, yes, but not appearance.'

'I think Dr Wrothby was able to effect a suitable disguise,' said Holmes. 'Is that so?'

'Meaney told me to do it,' said Shem. 'He said I could have part of the purse. It was good money, more than I had ever seen before, and —' He heaved a sigh so deep it must have hurt. 'I had seen Bella — she worked as a clerk in a lettings agency, quite near — and I thought, that little lady, she is the one for me, but I never had the courage to even speak to her. I thought maybe, if I had a little money, I might be able to court her.

'I didn't want to fight Arroway. I didn't even think I could, and the company would know I wasn't Lunn, but then Wrothby said he would put a bandage around my head to cover my hair, and dab blood on my face. They didn't give me a chance to say no. The next thing I knew, they had got me ready and pushed me into the ring. I'm not too clever on my feet, and the crowd all yelled that I was drunk. And Arroway laughed at me, but then — I think seeing me close up, he knew. He stared at me, and then he shouted out, "This is all wrong! I know you! You are no boxer! You are —" and I suppose I panicked. I closed my eyes and just lashed out. I must have hit him hard. When I opened my eyes, he was lying there.

'Then Dr Wrothby and Meaney and Baxter said they would make it all right. They would take Lunn home and say it was him in the fight and not me, and say he hurt his wrist hitting Arroway, and he would have to lie low for a bit.' Shem looked at Holmes. 'I'm sorry, Mr Holmes. Baxter said he would be able to bribe you to keep quiet. I didn't know what he meant to do.'

Professor Logan sat staring at his miserable younger brother. 'I don't know what to say,' he said at last. 'If you had spun me that tale, Holmes, I wouldn't have believed it, but with Shem saying it, well, it can't be denied. I just can't think what is best to be done, now.'

Shem sat upright. 'I've lived with this guilt for years,' he said, 'but it's time to bring it into the open. If Bella won't want me now, then it must be what I deserve. You say, Holmes, that you have seen Lunn? He has had that guilt to live with too, so he needs to know the truth. I'm going to go and talk to Bella now, and then I shall go to the police and confess.'

CHAPTER FORTY-ONE

I was unsurprised when I learned that Mrs Shem, a sensible lady, had recognised that there was no malice in the actions of her contrite husband. She supported his determination to confess, knowing that it would bring him peace. Shem Logan was charged with manslaughter but was granted bail while awaiting trial. His presence behind the bar of the King Henry aroused some curiosity in the boxing world, but he refused to publicly discuss the fight which had led to the death of Matthew Arroway. As a part of his penance, however, he sought an introduction to Mr Lunn, and in a private conversation told him all the details of that night. In a separate conversation he revealed his shame to Mrs Arroway and Miss Mitchell, saying that he would accept whatever punishment the court awarded.

'So, your enquiries are concluded,' I said to Holmes when we next spoke. 'And a strange set of cases it has been. Bowman died from natural disease, Summers from misadventure, and Arroway's death was manslaughter, for which Shem Logan was not entirely responsible, so we can hope the jury will be lenient. Not a murder amongst them.'

'Yes, there is one,' said Holmes, 'and one which I cannot bring home to the perpetrator. It is a hard thing, Stamford, to be in possession of the truth but unable to express it as anything other than a theory. Murder has been done, I have no doubt of it, but I have no proof. Only a confession will bring the guilty to justice, and I doubt that it will be forthcoming since the murderer feels not one jot of regret. I have done all I can.'

'Please tell me, Holmes.'

'I have little doubt that the unlamented Dr Wrothby was murdered.'

'By his wife, you mean? I agree, that would be hard to prove. She was seen with him that night, when he came home drunk, but she didn't strike him. Oh!' I exclaimed. 'Sally saw her speak to him, but from an attic window she could not have seen all that occurred. Supposing she administered a drug by needle, and Dr Goode did not notice the mark?'

'He was not murdered by his wife. His killer was Walter Robson.'

'But what reason would Robson have to do that? He even threatened me when I wanted to find Mrs Wrothby.'

'Not to protect the lady, to protect himself.'

'How did Wrothby die?'

'A single blow to the temple. It must have been almost instant. Robson lifted the body into the chaise, put the reins in the hands and set the horse on its way. It knew its way home; it had taken its master home drunk many a time, and this time was very little different. At the inquest, Dr Goode was eager to suggest that Wrothby had died in the chaise soon after arriving home. I think he wanted to protect the widow from any hint of blame. He made light of the appearance of bruises, even the one that was recent, the slight red mark.'

'But why did Robson strike Wrothby?'

'Recall that Wrothby was in a maudlin mood that night. He said there was something he had done for which he needed forgiveness. He told no-one what this was, but when Robson guided him to the chaise, they were briefly alone in the coach yard. I think that was when he made his confession and asked to be forgiven. Recall that this happened after a night of drinking when Robson would not have been sober, but Professor Logan commented that Robson appeared sober when he returned from the coach yard. What sobered him? Did Wrothby reveal something that came as a shock? I think he did. Why did he confess only to Robson? And why did Robson kill him?'

I waited to be told.

'There was only one revelation that could have shocked Robson and led him to murder Wrothby. The great sadness in Robson's life was the death of his wife. She suffered almost constant pain from a back injury, and was tended by Dr Wrothby, who prescribed strong drugs to give her ease. I think that Wrothby, possibly while under the influence of drink, made an error in the dose that caused her to die before her time. I have found no evidence that there was ever a post-mortem examination, something which ought to have been ordered if the death was sudden, even after a long illness. Wrothby took on the task of making all the arrangements, supposedly as a service to his friend, but in reality, to cover up his guilt. He certified her death as failure of the heart, and as he had been the attending doctor for some years, this was never questioned.

'Recall what Robson told Professor Logan after seeing Wrothby on his way? He said he had told Wrothby that the Almighty would forgive him, and then he put him in the chaise. He knew that the man was dead and was about to appear before his maker for judgement.'

'Do you think he meant to kill?'

'One blow to the temple from a seasoned pugilist. He knew what he was doing.'

'So, when Mrs Wrothby found her husband, he was already dead?'

'Quite probably. The heart would have stopped, but the body would still have been warm. Was he beyond being revived? I can't say. Such things have been known in rare cases. Another woman finding her husband in that condition would have done something to try and restore him. I am sure she knew what to do, but she did not.'

'She just left him sitting there all night.'

'Yes. I think she wanted to make sure.'

I thought about Holmes's dilemma. 'There is nothing you can do. Any suggestion that Wrothby was murdered would only direct attention to the widow. It might be alleged that she found her husband drunk and struck him with something.'

'Sally's observation proves that she did not, but I am afraid that the testimony of a servant girl looking out of an attic window in the dark will not count for a great deal.'

EPILOGUE

At Shem Logan's subsequent trial for the manslaughter of Matthew Arroway, defence counsel told the court that his client was coerced into the fight by his employer, had no skill at boxing, and lashed out with his eyes closed, unnerved when the other man taunted him. It was admitted that Arroway's death was due to the events of that bout, not so much the blow itself, but the impact of the unconscious man's head as he fell, but it was maintained that the defendant had never intended to injure the other man. The main instigators were Wrothby and Meaney, who were both dead, and Harry Baxter, who was in prison having been found guilty of the attempted murder of a student of Barts Medical College. Even if the Arroway fight was declared illegal, this was not, it was argued, the fault of Shem Logan, who was no more than an instrument of his employer. Shem was acquitted.

Jim Jones returned to Cornwall, where he assisted his father in his metalsmiths business while he considered his future. His father had become very busy in recent years with the repair of bicycles and while Jones was so occupied, he had an idea for a modification to the design which would improve performance. He went on to create his own wholly original bicycle, which attracted considerable custom from racing enthusiasts. Eventually he opened a business manufacturing bicycles which proved to be very successful and was occasionally to be seen riding in displays and races. On sunny afternoons, he and his wife took to the country lanes in a sociable, a bicycling equipage for two, operating the treadles as they sat side by side.

Walter Robson was never charged with the murder of Dr Wrothby, which remained in the annals of boxing as a natural death. Holmes and I often wondered how much Professor Logan really knew about what had happened that night, but even if he had suspected his old friend, he owed him too much to do anything other than protect him. We later discovered that Dr Wrothby had told the Logans that he had wanted to order an inquest on Mrs Robson, but that the distraught husband had begged him not to as he could not bear to think of his wife's body being cut up. Holmes's observation on being told this was that he rather thought the truth was the other way about, and it was Wrothby who did not want to have the cause of death too closely examined.

Robson spent his remaining days in quiet contemplation of his sins, occasionally arguing with the persistent ghost of Dr Wrothby. A few years later, he passed away very suddenly. Kindness said that a weak heart was to blame, but it was not hard to imagine that Dr Wrothby had at last exacted his revenge.

The Ladies' Anti-pugilism League had a great fight on its hands, not least because of the opposition and derision of men, many of whom were unable to appreciate that the members of the League were concerned with the well-being of their menfolk and families. If these cavillers gave the movement any thought at all, they assumed that once the ladies married and were occupied with homes and babies then all that anti-boxing nonsense would stop. The League, however, was not to be intimidated or suppressed. It enjoyed the strong leadership of Miss Mitchell, while Mrs Arroway, who married the repentant Mr Lunn, continued to offer her support. The League still exists in some form to this day, having passed through a variety of guises, encouraging, and eventually amalgamating with other worthy organisations.

While it has never succeeded in its aim of banning boxing altogether, it has been a valuable and important force to improve measures to protect boxers against injury, ensure better compliance with the rules, and provide support for families affected by the loss or injury of a loved one.

Mr and Mrs Lunn went on to became important figures in the temperance movement and appeared together at numerous events dispensing tea and wisdom. Their lectures drew large crowds and raised substantial funds for charity. Mrs Goode, unsure if she could ever be forgiven her deception, and not wanting to find out, took a step back from the League, and continued her charitable works with other agencies.

After witnessing the confrontation of Miss Mitchell and Professor Logan, I had wondered if there was to be an announcement forthcoming. It was apparent that he was impressed with the lady, and since she had been disappointed of a connection with Butcher Blunt, a reciprocal interest was not beyond the bounds of possibility. I did learn that from that time onwards, the professor assisted the campaigning ladies of the League with recommendations for improving the safety of boxing, and that his initial meeting with Miss Mitchell was not the only one. There was even a rumour that he had offered to make her his third wife, but she had declined, mainly on the grounds that his first two were still living.

The great figures of those tumultuous days of boxing are gone, now. Jem Mace, once a wealthy man, sadly gambled away his fortune and died a pauper in 1910. Bob Travers died at a great age, a revered figure in 1918. I have heard little of Professor

Logan in recent years, but the King Henry Tavern still thrives, although Mr and Mrs Shem Logan retired in peaceful harmony to a more rural location, leaving its management to their sons. I like to imagine the professor nowadays in a contented old age, still overseeing his domain, and enjoying the respect he rightly deserves.

Not long after the events of that winter of 1876, Holmes was invited to luncheon by the Marquess of Queensberry and his sporting friend John Graham Chambers, the man who formulated the Queensberry Rules. Holmes's work in exposing some of the bad elements in sport had not gone unnoticed, and there was a lively conversation about advancing the legal status of professional boxing. Holmes was still no more than a youthful student, a dilettante in the art of detection. He was not yet the chosen man to investigate the delicate private affairs of the crowned heads of Europe, but he had attracted the interest of the nobility, and had stepped onto the path that would lead to his later fame.

HISTORICAL NOTES

In the 1870s the West London Boxing Club met in a large room in the Bedford Head Hotel, Maiden Lane, Covent Garden. That public house has since been renamed the Maple Leaf. My description of the King Henry Tavern is inspired by the size and location of the Maple Leaf but is not intended to be that public house.

Graham Gordon's *Master of the Ring* is an extensive and informative biography of the 'father of boxing' Jem Mace, (1831–1910), whose career spanned the period from the prize ring to the establishment of boxing as a legal sport. Mace, while humbly born in Norfolk, and uneducated, had several things in common with Holmes. He was an all-round athlete who also fenced and played the violin. Mace recognised a commonality between fencing — the targeted thrusts of the foil and the blows of the sabre — and the punches of the boxer, and I have taken the liberty of having Holmes make the same connection.

Singlestick is a martial art using wooden swords, which originated from the training of soldiers in swordsmanship. Watson declared Holmes to be an expert singlestick player as well as an excellent boxer and swordsman.

'Assault at Arms' was the name given to the kind of martial arts exhibition described by Luckhurst in chapter 1. The expression had largely fallen into disuse by the 1960s.

The Royal Agricultural Hall was opened in 1862, its principal purpose being to host exhibitions of livestock and agricultural machinery. Before long, its space was leased to host large-scale entertainments and sporting competitions. The building now houses the Business Design centre.

In Greek mythology the Furies are deities of vengeance, usually three in number.

In 1876/7, when this novel is set, the Marquess of Queensberry, aged thirty-two, was a popular supporter of sports, chiefly horse racing, boxing, athletics and cricket, and his reputation for eccentricity had not yet arisen. For a detailed biography I refer the reader to my *The Marquess of Queensberry: Wilde's Nemesis* (Yale University Press 2013).

Bob Travers was born in America in 1832 and brought to England when two years of age. His father is said to have run a shop in Truro, Cornwall, selling crockery. By 1855 he was attracting attention as a promising young boxer. He was 5ft 5 inches tall with a strong build. A popular competitor, described in the press as tough, gallant, and doughty, he was known as the 'Black Wonder,' and the 'Ebony Gentleman'. He retired in the 1860s but continued to teach boxing and give sparring demonstrations. He died in Wandsworth in 1918. (*Evening Despatch*, 14 December 1918).

From 1838 to 1867 the sport of boxing was governed by the London Prize Ring rules. There was no limit on the number of rounds, a round ended when a man was knocked down, and the match ended when one boxer was unable to continue.

The Marquess of Queensberry Rules were so called because they were introduced for the competitions for the Queensberry cups, sponsored by the Marquess. They were published in 1867, having been drafted by the Marquess's friend, Welsh sportsman and founder of many popular sporting competitions, John Graham Chambers, (1843–1883). The rules stipulated the wearing of padded gloves and that rounds were to last no longer than three minutes, and introduced the count of ten for a fallen man.

Boxers were sometimes charged with manslaughter after an opponent's death. An example of this is the case of boxer John Young, who was tried for manslaughter following the death of Edward Wilmot. The landlord of the premises and four seconds were tried as accomplices. The trial took place at the Old Bailey on 19 November 1866. Inevitably, the legality and risks of boxing were an important subject of debate. The trial details can be found at https://www.oldbaileyonline.org, reference number t18661119-44.

The question of the legality of boxing is discussed in an article in *The Sporting Times*, 15 November 1890 p. 2. Two boxers, Slavin and McAuliffe, had been arrested earlier that month and charged with assault and committing a breach of the peace, following a match at the Ormonde Club. After a jury was unable to agree on a verdict, the prosecution was withdrawn. The patronage of the fifth Earl of Lonsdale was influential in the eventual acceptance of regulated boxing as legal.

Jim Jones's words are an echo of comments in *Defence of Pugilism*, published in volume 2 of *Pugilistica* pp 479–81. The theme of the argument was that pugilism did not, as had been claimed, have a brutalising effect on gallant Britons, who were characterised by a thinking rather than a frenzied courage. 'Fair play is a Briton's motto; we would extend it to the extremities of the earth, no consequence what country, religion, or colour. The sable African, throwing aside the chains that levelled him with the beast, now walks erect, in the majesty of freedom and liberty, calling down blessings on the country that in spite of all the world, burst his bonds asunder.'

Risus sardonicus, the sardonic grin, is a characteristic appearance seen soon after death from tetanus and strychnine poisoning as a result of convulsions. In *A Study in Scarlet* Holmes is faced with the corpse of a poisoned man, the face similarly contorted, and deduces from this that the deceased was in a state of terror before his death.

William James Russell (1830–1909) was an English chemist and Fellow of the Royal Society. From 1870 to 1897 he was professor and lecturer in chemistry at Barts.

Easton's Syrup was a popular nervine and general tonic, the active ingredients being iron phosphate, quinine, and strychnine. It had a bitter taste and was also available in pill form.

Holmes was well acquainted with the notorious Palmer poisoning case, which he refers to in *The Adventure of the Speckled Band*.

The volume on poisons consulted by Stamford may well have been *Principles of Forensic Medicine* by William A. Guy and David Ferrier. The fourth edition was published in 1875.

A grain is one of the smallest units of measurement ever commonly used. It is equivalent to 0.065 of a gram.

Stamford's memoirs were written in 1924, so his mention of current use of strychnine refers to that year. Strychnine triggers nerve spasms which were once thought to be a stimulus to the system. It is now understood that this is not beneficial, and it is no longer prescribed for medicinal use. The author, a former chemists' dispenser, recalls selling strychnine to licensed pest controllers in the 1960s, and tincture of nux vomica was then an ingredient of mixtures made in the dispensary. In Europe, strychnine was banned from use in agriculture and rodent control in 2006.

'Sherrinford' was a name Conan Doyle considered for Holmes before settling on Sherlock.

The registers of births, marriages and deaths were held at Somerset House in London until 1970.

Holmes, as chronicled in *The Adventure of the Final Problem*, published in December 1893, disappeared from the Reichenbach Falls in May 1891, after which some enthusiasts of his adventures were seen wearing black armbands. Holmes was assumed to be dead until the publication of *The Adventure of the Empty House* in 1903, which revealed that he had returned to London in April 1894.

The Christian Mission was originally founded as the East London Christian Mission in 1865 by William and Catherine Booth. It was renamed The Salvation Army in 1878.

Bell's Life in London and Sporting Chronicle was published from 1822–1886. In the 1870s *Fistiana, or the Oracle of the Ring* was published at the paper's office in Strand, London, price 3s 6d.

It was not until 1912 that the index books of marriages recorded the surname of the spouse.

A NOTE TO THE READER

The timeline of the events in the life of Sherlock Holmes in the canonical fifty-six stories and four novels has occupied, fascinated and sometimes frustrated Holmesian scholars for many years. The most commonly accepted year of Holmes' birth is 1854. He did not meet Dr Watson and occupy 221b Baker Street before 1881.

Almost nothing is known about his early life and very little about his education. I think it is possible that, like Conan Doyle, he spent a year at school on the continent, where he acquired his knowledge of modern languages. He is known to have spent two years at a collegiate university, which means either Oxford or Cambridge, although which one, and what courses he took have never been revealed, but he did not take a degree. The year in which he settled permanently in London is unspecified. His first recorded case is that of "The Adventure of the *Gloria Scott*", as recounted to Dr Watson, which took place during the university vacation. Holmes had been developing his powers of observation and deduction and was known amongst fellow students for his singular method of analysing problems. At the time this was nothing more to him than an intellectual exercise. During his work on the *Gloria Scott* mystery, however, it was suggested to him that he would make a brilliant detective and that idea took hold and gave him a direction in life.

Holmes realised that he lacked the broad and varied fields of knowledge which would serve as a foundation for his mental skills. The next few years were dedicated to acquiring that knowledge, and in doing so, he created the man who burst upon the literary scene and met Dr Watson in the first Holmes novel, *A Study in Scarlet*.

In my work, I have suggested that Holmes was at university during the years 1873–75, solving the *Gloria Scott* mystery after his second year. Realising that his particular requirements could not be provided by a university course, he did not return, choosing instead to undertake his own studies. He had boxed and fenced at university and while there is no evidence that he devoted dedicated practice to either later on, it is clear that these were skills he retained. His lodgings in London's Montague Street placed him close to the British Museum where he must have spent many hours studying in the library, and he enrolled at St Bartholomew's Medical College for practical courses in chemistry and anatomy.

And that is where my series begins.

Reviews are so important to authors, and if you enjoyed the novel I would be grateful if you could spare a few minutes to post a review on **Amazon** and **Goodreads**. I love hearing from readers, and you can connect with me online, **on Facebook**, **Twitter**, and **Instagram**.

You can also stay up to date with all my news via **my website** and by signing up to **my newsletter**.

Linda Stratmann

2022

lindastratmann.com

Sapere Books is an exciting new publisher of brilliant fiction and popular history.

To find out more about our latest releases and our monthly bargain books visit our website: **saperebooks.com**

Printed in Great Britain
by Amazon